HORRiD HENRY'S
Jolly
Holidays

Francesca Simon
Illustrated by Tony Ross

Orion
Children's Books

ORION CHILDREN'S BOOKS
This collection first published in Great Britain in 2017
by Hodder and Stoughton
1 3 5 7 9 10 8 6 4 2

Text © Francesca Simon 1999, 2007, 2008,
2009, 2010, 2011, 2012, 2013, 2014, 2015, 2016
Illustrations © Tony Ross 1999, 2007, 2008,
2009, 2010, 2011, 2012, 2013, 2014, 2015, 2016
Puzzles and activities © Orion Children's Books, 2017

The moral right of the author and illustrator have been asserted.

ISBN 978 1 5101 0235 4

Printed and bound in Great Britain by Clays Ltd, St Ives plc

The paper and board used in this book are from well-managed forests
and other responsible sources.

Orion Children's Books
An imprint of
Hachette Children's Books
Part of Hodder and Stoughton
Carmelite House
50 Victoria Embankment
London EC4Y 0DZ

An Hachette UK Company
www.hachette.co.uk
www.hachettechildrens.co.uk
www.horridhenry.co.uk

HORRiD HENRY'S
Jolly Holidays

Francesca Simon spent her childhood on the beach
in California, and then went to Yale and Oxford
Universities to study medieval history and literature.
She now lives in London with her family. She has written
over 50 books and won the Children's Book of the Year
at the Galaxy British Book Awards for *Horrid Henry and
the Abominable Snowman*.

Tony Ross is one of the most popular and successful
of all children's illustrators, with almost 50 picture books
to his name. He has also produced line drawings for
many fiction titles, for authors such as David Walliams,
Enid Blyton, Astrid Lindgren and many more.

For a complete list of **Horrid Henry** titles
see the end of the book, or visit
www.horridhenry.co.uk

or

www.orionchildrensbooks.co.uk

CONTENTS

HORRID HENRY AND THE DINNER GUESTS

FIZZ! POP! GURGLE! BANG!

Horrid Henry sat on the kitchen floor watching his new Dungeon Drink kit brew a bubbly purple potion.

BELCH! CRUNCH! OOZE! SPLAT!

Beside it, a Grisly Ghoul Grub box heaved and spewed some Rotten Crispies.

Dad dashed into the kitchen.

'Want a crisp?' said Henry, smirking.

'No!' said Dad, putting on his apron. 'And I've told you before to play with

1

those disgusting kits in your bedroom.'

Why Henry's grandmother had bought him those terrible toys for Christmas he would never know.

'Henry, I want you to listen carefully,' said Dad, feverishly rolling out pastry. 'Mum's new boss and her husband are coming to dinner in an hour. I want total cooperation and perfect behaviour.'

'Yeah, yeah,' said Henry, his eyes glued to the frothing machine.

Horrid Henry's parents didn't have guests for dinner very often. The last time they did Henry had sneaked downstairs, eaten the entire chocolate cake Dad had baked for dessert and then been sick all over the sofa. The time before that he'd put whoopee cushions on all the guests' seats, bitten Peter, and broken the banister by sliding down it.

2

PRRRRP

Dad started getting pots and pans down.

'What are you cooking?' said Perfect Peter, tidying up his stamps.

'Salmon wrapped in pastry with lime and ginger,' said Dad, staring at his list.

'Yummy!' said Perfect Peter. 'My favourite!'

'Yuck!' said Horrid Henry. 'I want

pizza. What's for pudding?'

'Chocolate mousse,' said Dad.

'Can I help?' said Peter.

'Of course,' said Mum, smiling.

'You can pass round the nuts and crisps when Mr and Mrs Mossy arrive.'

Nuts? Crisps? Henry's ears perked up.

'I'll help too,' said Henry.

Mum looked at him. 'We'll see,' she said.

'I don't think Henry should pass round the nuts,' said Peter. 'He'll only eat them himself.'

'Shut up, Peter,' snarled Henry.

'Mum! Henry told me to shut up!' wailed Peter.

'Henry! Stop being horrid,' muttered Dad, grating ginger and squeezing limes.

While Dad rolled up salmon in pastry, Mum dashed about setting the table with the best china.

'Hey! You haven't set enough places,' said Henry. 'You've only set the table for four.'

'That's right,' said Mum. 'Mrs Mossy, Mr Mossy, Dad and me.'

'What about me?' said Henry.

'And me?' said Peter.

'This is a grown-ups' party,' said Mum.

'You want me . . . to go . . . to bed?' Henry stuttered. 'I'm not . . . eating with you?'

'No,' said Dad.

'It's not fair!' shrieked Henry. 'What am I having for supper then?'

'A cheese sandwich,' said Dad. 'We've got to get ready for the guests. I'm already two minutes behind my schedule.'

'I'm not eating this swill!' shrieked Henry, shoving the sandwich off his plate. 'I want pizza!'

'That's all right, Dad,' said Peter, tucking into his sandwich. 'I understand that grown-ups need to be by themselves sometimes.'

Henry lunged at Peter. He was a cannibal trussing his victim for the pot.

'AAARGHH!' shrieked Peter.

'That's it, Henry, go to bed!' shouted Mum.

'I won't!' screamed Henry. 'I want chocolate mousse!'

'Go upstairs and stay upstairs!' shouted Mum.

Ding dong!

'Aaagh!' squealed Dad. 'They're early! I haven't finished the mousse yet.'

Horrid Henry stomped upstairs to his bedroom and slammed the door.

He was so angry he could hardly speak. The injustice of it all. Why

6

should he go to bed while Mum and
Dad were downstairs having fun and
eating chocolate mousse? The delicious
smell of melting chocolate wafted into
his nostrils. Henry's tummy rumbled. If
Mum and Dad thought he'd stay in bed
while they all had fun downstairs they
had rocks for brains.

SCREEEECH! SCREEEECH!

Perfect Peter must be playing his
cello for Mum and Dad and the guests.
Which meant . . . Horrid Henry smiled.
The coast was clear. Hello, nuts, here
I come, thought Henry.

Henry tip-toed downstairs. The
screechy-scratchy sounds continued
from the sitting room.

Horrid Henry sneaked into the empty
kitchen. There were the bowls of nuts
and crisps and the drinks all ready to
serve.

Cashews, my favourite. I'll just have
a few, he thought.

Chomp. Chomp. Chomp.

Hmmn, boy, those nuts were good.
Irresistible, really, thought Henry. A few
more would go down a treat. And, if he
poured the remaining nuts into a smaller
bowl, no one would notice how many

he'd eaten.

CHOMP! CHOMP! CHOMP!

Just one more, thought Henry, and that's it.

Horrid Henry swizzled his fingers round the nut bowl.

Uh-oh. There were only three nuts left.

Yikes, thought Henry. Now I'm in trouble.

FIZZ! POP! GURGLE! BANG! BELCH! CRUNCH! OOZE! SPLAT!

Horrid Henry looked at his Grisly Grub box and Dungeon Drink kit and bopped himself on the head. What an idiot he was. What better time to try out his grisly grub than . . . now?

Henry examined the Rotten Crispies he'd made earlier. They looked like crisps, but certainly didn't taste like them. The only problem was, what to do with the good crisps?

Yum yum! thought Henry, crunching crisps as fast as he could. Then he re-filled the bowl with Rotten Crispies.

Next, Henry poured two frothing dungeon drinks into glasses, and put them on the tray.

Perfect, thought Henry. Now to make some Nasty Nuts to replace all those cashews.

The kitchen door opened. Dad came in.

'What are you doing, Henry? I told you to go to bed.'

'Mum said I could serve the nuts,' said Henry, lying shamelessly. Then he grabbed the two bowls and escaped.

The sound of applause came from
the sitting room. Perfect Peter bowed
modestly.

'Isn't he adorable?' said Mrs Mossy.

'And so talented,' said Mr Mossy.

'Hello, Mr and Mrs Bossy,' said
Henry.

Mum looked horrified.

'Mossy, not Bossy, dear,' said Mum.

'But that's what *you* call them, Mum,'
said Henry, smiling sweetly.

'Henry is just going to bed,' said Mum, blushing.

'No I wasn't,' said Henry. 'I was going to serve the nuts and crisps. Don't you remember?'

'Oooh, I love nuts,' said Mrs Mossy.

'I told you to stay upstairs,' hissed Mum.

'Muuuum,' wailed Peter. 'You said I could serve the guests.'

'You can serve the crisps, Peter,' said Henry graciously, handing him the bowl of Rotten Crispies. 'Would you like a cashew, Mrs Bossy?'

'Mossy!' hissed Mum.

'Ooh, cashews, my favourite,' said Mrs Mossy. She plunged her fingers into the mostly empty nut bowl, and finally scooped up the remaining three.

Henry snatched two back.

'You're only supposed to have one

13

nut at a time,' he said. 'Don't be
greedy.'

'Henry!' said Mum. 'Don't be rude.'

'Want a nut?' said Henry, waving the
bowl in front of Mr Mossy.

'Why, yes, I . . .' said Mr Mossy.

But he was too late. Henry had
already moved away to serve Mum.

'Want a nut?' he asked.

Mum's hand reached out to take one, but Henry quickly whisked the bowl away.

'Henry!' said Mum.

'Do have some crisps, Mrs Mossy,' said Perfect Peter. Mrs Mossy scooped up a large handful of Rotten Crispies and then stuffed them in her mouth.

Her face went purple, then pink, then green.

'BLEEEEECH!' she spluttered, spitting them out all over Mr Mossy.

'Peter, run and get Mrs Mossy something to drink!' shouted Mum.

Peter dashed to the kitchen and brought back a frothing drink.

'Thank you,' gasped Mrs Mossy, taking the glass and gulping it down.

'YUCK!' she spluttered, spitting it out. 'Are you trying to poison me, you horrible child?' she choked, flailing her arms and crashing into Dad, who had just walked in carrying the drinks tray.

CRASH! SPLASH!

Mum, Dad, Peter, and Mr and Mrs Mossy were soaked.

'Peter, what have you done?' shouted Mum.

Perfect Peter burst into tears and ran out of the room.

'Oh dear, I'm so sorry,' said Mum.

'Never mind,' said Mrs Mossy,
through gritted teeth.

'Sit down, everyone,' said Henry. 'I'm
going to do a show now.'

'No,' said Mum.

'No,' said Dad.

'But Peter did one,' howled Henry. 'I
WANT TO DO A SHOW!'

'All right,' said Mum. 'But just a quick
one.'

Henry sang. The guests held their ears.

'Not so loud, Henry,' said Mum.

Henry pirouetted, trampling on the
guests.

'Ooof,' said Mr Mossy, clutching his
toe.

'Aren't you finished, Henry?' said
Dad.

Henry juggled, dropping both balls on
Mrs Mossy's head.

'Ow,' said Mrs Mossy.

'Now I'll show you my new karate moves,' said Henry.

'NO!' shouted Mum and Dad.

But before anyone could stop him Henry's arms and legs flew out in a mad karate dance.

'HI-YA!' shrieked Henry, knocking into Mr Mossy.

Mr Mossy went flying across the room. Whoosh! Off flew his toupee.

Click-clack! Out bounced his false teeth.

'Reginald!' gasped Mrs Mossy. 'Are you all right? Speak to me!'

'Uggghhh,' groaned Mr Mossy.

'Isn't that great?' said Henry. 'Who wants to go next?'

'What's that terrible smell?' choked Mrs Mossy.

'Oh no!' screamed Dad. 'The salmon is burning!'

Mum and Dad ran into the kitchen, followed by Mr and Mrs Mossy.

19

Smoke poured from the oven. Mum grabbed a tea towel and started whacking the burning salmon.

WHACK! THWACK!

'Watch out!' screamed Dad.

The towel thwacked the bowl of chocolate mousse and sent it crashing to the ground.

SPLAT! There was chocolate mousse on the floor. There was chocolate mousse on the ceiling. And there was chocolate mousse all over Mr and Mrs Mossy, Mum, Dad and Henry.

'Oh no,' said Mum, holding her head in her hands. Then she burst into tears. 'What are we going to do?'

'Leave it to me, Mum,' said Horrid Henry. He marched to the phone.

'Pizza Delight?' he said. 'I'd like to order a mega-whopper, please.'

Henry's Holiday Howlers

What do you get if
you eat the Christmas
decorations?
Tinselitis.

What's a cow's favourite
day of the year?
MOO Year's Day!

What food do you get if you cross
a snowman with a polar bear?
A brrr-grrr.

Why did Santa have to close his factory?
For elf and safety.

Where did the mistletoe go to become rich and famous?
Hollywood.

BRAINY BRIAN: What's the difference between an elephant and a postbox?
BEEFY BERT: I dunno.
BRAINY BRIAN: Well, I'm not asking you to post my Christmas cards.

HORRID HENRY'S HIKE

Horrid Henry looked out of the window. AAARRRGGGHHH! It was a lovely day. The sun was shining. The birds were tweeting. The breeze was blowing. Little fluffy clouds floated by in a bright blue sky.

Rats.

Why couldn't it be raining? Or hailing? Or sleeting?

Any minute, any second, it would happen . . . the words he'd been dreading, the words he'd give anything

not to hear, the words –

'Henry! Peter! Time to go for a walk,' called Mum.

'Yippee!' said Perfect Peter. 'I can wear my new yellow wellies!'

'NO!' screamed Horrid Henry.

Go for a walk! Go for a walk! Didn't he walk enough already? He walked to school. He walked home from school. He walked to the TV. He walked to the computer. He walked to the sweet jar *and* all the way back to the comfy black chair. Horrid Henry walked

plenty. Ugghh. The last thing he needed was more walking. More chocolate, yes. More crisps, yes. More *walking*? No way! Why oh why couldn't his parents ever say, 'Henry! Time to play on the computer.' Or 'Henry, stop doing your homework this minute! Time to turn on the TV.'

But no. For some reason his mean, horrible parents thought he spent too much time sitting indoors. They'd been threatening for weeks to make him go on a family walk. Now the dreadful moment had come. His precious weekend was ruined.

Horrid Henry hated nature. Horrid Henry hated fresh air. What could be more boring than walking up and down streets staring at lamp posts? Or sloshing across some stupid muddy park? Nature smelled. Uggh! He'd much rather be inside watching TV.

Mum stomped into the sitting room.

'Henry! Didn't you hear me calling?'

'No,' lied Henry.

'Get your wellies on, we're going,' said Dad, rubbing his hands. 'What a lovely day.'

'I don't want to go for a walk,' said Henry. 'I want to watch *Rapper Zapper Zaps Terminator Gladiator*.'

'But Henry,' said Perfect Peter, 'fresh air and exercise are so good for you.'

'I don't care!' shrieked Henry.

Horrid Henry stomped downstairs and flung open the front door. He breathed in deeply, hopped on one foot, then shut the door.

'There! Done it. Fresh air *and* exercise,' snarled Henry.

'Henry, we're going,' said Mum. 'Get in the car.'

Henry's ears pricked up.

'The car?' said Henry. 'I thought we were going for a walk.'

'We are,' said Mum. 'In the countryside.'

'Hurray!' said Perfect Peter. 'A nice *long* walk.'

'NOOOO!' howled Henry. Plodding along in the boring old park was bad enough, with its mouldy leaves and dog poo and stumpy trees. But at least the park wasn't very big. But the *countryside*?

The countryside was enormous! They'd be walking for hours, days, weeks, months, till his legs wore down to stumps and his feet fell off. And the countryside was so dangerous! Horrid Henry was sure he'd be swallowed up by quicksand or trampled to death by marauding chickens.

'I live in the city!' shrieked Henry. 'I don't want to go to the country!'

'Time you got out more,' said Dad.

'But look at those clouds,' moaned Henry, pointing to a fluffy wisp. 'We'll get soaked.'

'A little water never hurt anyone,' said Mum.

Oh yeah? Wouldn't they be sorry when he died of pneumonia.

'I'm staying here and that's final!' screamed Henry.

'Henry, we're waiting,' said Mum.

'Good,' said Henry.

'*I'm* all ready, Mum,' said Peter.

'I'm going to start deducting pocket money,' said Dad. '5p, 10p, 15p, 20 – '

Horrid Henry pulled on his wellies, stomped out of the door and got in the car. He slammed the door as hard as he could. It was so unfair! Why did he never get to do what *he* wanted to do? Now he would miss the first time Rapper Zapper had ever slugged it out with Terminator Gladiator. And all because he had to go on a long, boring, exhausting, horrible hike. He was so miserable he didn't even have the energy to kick Peter.

'Can't we just walk round the block?' moaned Henry.

'N-O spells no,' said Dad. 'We're going for a lovely walk in the countryside and that's that.'

Horrid Henry slumped miserably in his seat. Boy would they be sorry when he was gobbled up by goats. Boo hoo, if only we hadn't gone on that walk in the wilds, Mum would wail.

Henry was right, we should have listened to him, Dad would sob. I miss Henry, Peter would howl. I'll never eat goat's cheese again. And now it's too late, they would shriek.

If only, thought Horrid Henry. That would serve them right.

All too soon, Mum pulled into a carpark, on the edge of a small wood.

'Wow,' said Perfect Peter. 'Look at all those lovely trees.'

'Bet there are werewolves hiding there,' muttered Henry. 'And I hope they come and eat *you*!'

'Mum!' squealed Peter. 'Henry's trying to scare me.'

'Don't be horrid, Henry,' said Mum.

Horrid Henry looked around him. There was a gate, leading to endless meadows bordered by hedgerows. A muddy path wound through the trees and across the fields. A church spire stuck up in the distance.

'Right, I've seen the countryside, let's go home,' said Henry.

Mum glared at him.

'What?' said Henry, scowling.

'Let's enjoy this lovely day,' said Dad, sighing.

'So what do we do now?' said Henry.

'Walk,' said Dad.

'Where?' said Henry.

'Just walk,' said Mum, 'and enjoy the beautiful scenery.'

Henry groaned.

'We're heading for the lake,' said Dad, striding off. 'I've brought bread and we can feed the ducks.'

'But *Rapper Zapper* starts in an hour!'

'Tough,' said Mum.

Mum, Dad, and Peter headed through the gate into the field. Horrid Henry trailed behind them walking as slowly as he could.

'Ahh, breathe the lovely fresh air,' said Mum.

'We should do this more often,' said Dad.

Henry sniffed. The horrible smell of manure filled his nostrils.

'Ewww, smelly,' said Henry. 'Peter, couldn't you wait?'

'MUM!' shrieked Peter. 'Henry called me smelly.'

'Did not!'

'Did too!'

'Did not, smelly.'

'WAAAAAAAAA!' wailed Peter. 'Tell him to stop!'

'Don't be horrid, Henry!' screamed Mum. Her voice echoed. A dog walker passed her, and glared.

'Peter, would you rather run a mile, jump a stile, or eat a country pancake?' said Henry sweetly.

'Ooh,' said Peter. 'I love pancakes. And a country one must be even more delicious than a city one.'

'Ha ha,' cackled Horrid Henry, sticking out his tongue. 'Fooled you. Peter wants to eat cowpats!'

'MUM!' screamed Peter.

Henry walked.

And walked.

And walked.

His legs felt heavier, and heavier, and heavier.

'This field is muddy,' moaned Henry.

'I'm bored,' groaned Henry.

'My feet hurt,' whined Henry.

'Can't we go home? We've already walked miles,' whinged Henry.

'We've been walking for ten minutes,' said Dad.

'Please can we go on walks more often,' said Perfect Peter. 'Oh, look at those fluffy little sheepies!'

Horrid Henry pounced. He was a zombie biting the head off the hapless human.

'AAAAEEEEEE!' squealed Peter.

'Henry!' screamed Mum.

'Stop it!' screamed Dad. 'Or no TV for a week.'

When he was king, thought Horrid Henry, any parent who made their children go on a hike would be dumped barefoot in a scorpion-infested desert.

Plod.

Plod.

Plod.

Horrid Henry dragged his feet. Maybe his horrible mean parents would get fed up waiting for him and turn back, he thought, kicking some mouldy leaves.

Squelch.

Squelch.

Squelch.

Oh no, not *another* muddy meadow.

And then suddenly Horrid Henry had an idea. What was he thinking? All that fresh air must be rotting his brain. The sooner they got to the stupid lake, the sooner they could get home for the *Rapper Zapper Zaps Terminator Gladiator*.

'Come on, everyone, let's run!'

shrieked Henry. 'Race you down the
hill to the lake!'

'That's the spirit, Henry,' said Dad.

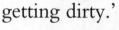

Horrid Henry dashed past
Dad.

'OW!' shrieked Dad,
tumbling into the
stinging nettles.

Horrid Henry whizzed past Mum.

'Eww!' shrieked Mum,
slipping in a cowpat.

Splat!

Horrid Henry
pushed past Peter.

'Waaa!' wailed Peter. 'My wellies are
getting dirty.'

39

Horrid Henry scampered down the muddy path.

'Wait Henry!' yelped Mum. 'It's too slipp – aaaiiieeeee!'

Mum slid down the path on her bottom.

'Slow down!' puffed Dad.

'I can't run that fast,' wailed Peter.

But Horrid Henry raced on.

'Shortcut across the field!' he called. 'Come on slowcoaches!' The black and white cow grazing alone in the middle raised its head.

'Henry!' shouted Dad.

Horrid Henry kept running.

'I don't think that's a cow!' shouted Mum.

The cow lowered its head and charged.

'It's a bull!' yelped Mum and Dad.
'RUN!'

'I said it was dangerous in the
countryside!' gasped Henry, as everyone
clambered over the stile in the nick of
time. 'Look, there's the lake!' he added,
pointing.

Henry ran down to the water's edge.
Peter followed. The embankment
narrowed to a point. Peter slipped past
Henry and bagged the best spot, right
at the water's edge where the ducks
gathered.

'Hey, get away from there,' said
Henry.

'I want to feed the ducks,' said Peter.

'*I* want to feed the ducks,' said Henry.
'Now move.'

'I was here first,' said Peter.

'Not any more,' said Henry.

Horrid Henry pushed Peter.

'Out of my way, worm!'

Perfect Peter pushed him back.

'Don't call me worm!'

Henry wobbled.

Peter wobbled.

Splash!

Peter tumbled into the lake.

Crash!

Henry tumbled into the lake.

'My babies!' shrieked Mum, jumping in after them.

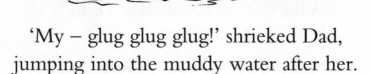

'My – glug glug glug!' shrieked Dad, jumping into the muddy water after her.

'My new wellies!' gurgled Perfect Peter.

Bang!

Pow!

Terminator Gladiator slashed at Rapper Zapper.

Zap!

Rapper Zapper slashed back.

'Go Zappy!' yelled Henry, lying bundled up in blankets on the sofa. Once everyone had scrambled out of the lake, Mum and Dad had been keen to get home as fast as possible.

'I think the park next time,' mumbled Dad, sneezing.

'Definitely,' mumbled Mum, coughing.

'Oh, I don't know,' said Horrid Henry happily. 'A little water never hurt anyone.'

Henry's Holiday Howlers

What do snowmen
call their offspring?
Chill-dren.

What do angry mice send
each other at Christmas?
Cross mouse cards.

What do you get if you cross a library
and an elf?
A shhh–elf.

What is Tarzan's favourite Christmas song?
Jungle Bells.

Why do reindeers wear fur coats?
Because they'd look silly in plastic macs.

What do vampires sing
on New Year's Eve?
Old Fang Syne.

What do snowmen eat for breakfast?
Snowflakes.

Why did the turkey
cross the road?
*It was the chicken's
day off.*

HORRiD HENRY ROBS THE BANK

'I want the skull!'

'I want the skull!'

'*I* want the skull!' said Horrid Henry, glaring.

'You had it last time, Henry,' said Perfect Peter. 'I *never* get it.'

'Did not.'

'Did too.'

'*I'm* the guest so I get the skull,' said Moody Margaret, snatching it from the box. '*You* can have the claw.'

'NOOOOOOOO!' wailed Henry.

'The skull is my lucky piece.'

Margaret looked smug. 'You know I'm going to win, Henry, 'cause I always do. So ha ha ha.'

'Wanna bet?' muttered Horrid Henry.

The good news was that Horrid Henry was playing *Gotcha*, the world's best board game. Horrid Henry loved *Gotcha*. You rolled the dice and travelled round the board, collecting treasure, buying dragon lairs and praying you didn't land in your enemies' lairs or in the Dungeon.

The bad news was that Horrid Henry was having to play *Gotcha* with his worm toad crybaby brother.

The worst news was that Moody Margaret, the world's biggest cheater, was playing with them. Margaret's mum was out for the afternoon, and had dumped Margaret at Henry's. Why oh

why did she have to play at his house?
Why couldn't her mum just dump her
in the bin where she belonged?

Unfortunately, the last time they'd
played *Gotcha*, Margaret had won. The
last two, three, four and five times
they'd played, Margaret had won.
Margaret was a demon *Gotcha* player.

Well, not any longer.

This time, Henry was determined to
beat her. Horrid Henry hated losing. By
hook or by crook, he would triumph.
Moody Margaret had beaten him at
Gotcha for the very last time.

49

'Who'll be banker?' said Perfect Peter.

'Me,' said Margaret.

'Me,' said Henry. Being in charge of all the game's treasure was an excellent way of topping up your coffers when none of the other players was looking.

'I'm the guest so *I'm* banker,' said Margaret. 'You can be the dragon keeper.'

Horrid Henry's hand itched to yank Margaret's hair. But then Margaret would scream and scream and Mum would send Henry to his room and

confiscate *Gotcha* until Henry was old and bald and dead.

'Touch any treasure that isn't yours, and you're dragon food,' hissed Henry.

'Steal any dragon eggs that aren't yours and you're toast,' hissed Margaret.

'If you're banker and Henry's the dragon keeper, what am I?' said Perfect Peter.

'A toad,' said Henry. 'And count yourself lucky.'

Horrid Henry snatched the dice. 'I'll go first.' The player who went first always had the best chance of buying up the best dragon lairs like Eerie Eyrie and Hideous Hellmouth.

'No,' said Margaret, 'I'll go first.'

'I'm the youngest, I should go first,' said Peter.

'Me!' said Margaret, snatching the dice. 'I'm the guest.'

'Me!' said Henry, snatching them back.

'Me!' said Peter.

'MUM!' screamed Henry and Peter.

Mum ran in. 'You haven't even started playing and already you're fighting,' said Mum.

'It's my turn to go first!' wailed Henry, Margaret, and Peter.

'The rules say to roll the dice and whoever gets the highest number goes first,' said Mum. 'End of story.' She left, closing the door behind her.

Henry rolled. Four. Not good.

'Peter's knee touched mine when I rolled the dice,' protested Henry. 'I get another turn.'

'No you don't,' said Margaret.

'Muuum! Henry's cheating!' shrieked
Peter.

'If I get called one more time,'
screamed Mum from upstairs, 'I will
throw that game in the bin.'

Eeeek.

Margaret rolled. Three.

'You breathed on me,' hissed Margaret.

'Did not,' said Henry.

'Did too,' said Margaret. 'I get another
go.'

'No way,' said Henry.

Peter picked up the dice.

'Low roll, low roll, low roll,' chanted
Henry.

'Stop it, Henry,' said Peter.

'Low roll, low roll, low roll,' chanted

53

Henry louder.

Peter rolled an eleven.

'Yippee, I go first,' trilled Peter.

Henry glared at him.

Perfect Peter took a deep breath, and rolled the dice to start the game.

Five. A Fate square.

Perfect Peter moved his gargoyle to the Fate square and picked up a Fate card. Would it tell him to claim a treasure hoard, or send him to the Dungeon? He squinted at it.

'The og . . . the ogr . . . I can't read it,' he said. 'The words are too hard for me.'

Henry snatched the card. It read:

The Ogres make you king for a day. Collect 20 rubies from the other players.

'The Ogres make you king for a day. Give 20 rubies to the player on your left,' read Henry. 'And that's me, so pay up.'

Perfect Peter handed Henry twenty rubies.

Tee hee, thought Horrid Henry.

'I think you read that Fate card wrong, Henry,' said Moody Margaret grimly.

Uh oh. If Margaret read Peter the card, he was dead. Mum would make them stop playing, and Henry would get into trouble. Big, big trouble.

'Didn't,' said Henry.

'Did,' said Margaret. 'I'm telling on you.'

Horrid Henry looked at the card again. 'Whoops. Silly me. I read it too fast,' said Henry. 'It says, give 20 rubies to *all* the other players.'

'Thought so,' said Moody Margaret.

Perfect Peter rolled the dice. Nine! Oh no, that took Peter straight to Eerie

Eyrie, Henry's favourite lair. Now Peter
could buy it. Everyone always landed on
it and had to pay ransom or get eaten.
Rats, rats, rats.

'1, 2, 3, 4, 5, 6, 7, 8, 9, look, Henry,
I've landed on Eerie Eyrie
and no one owns it
yet,' said Peter.
'Don't buy it,'
said Henry.
'It's the worst
lair on the
board. No one   ever lands on it. You'd
just be wasting your money.'

'Oh,' said Peter. He looked doubtful.

'But . . . but . . .' said Peter.

'Save your money for when you land
in other people's lairs,' said Henry.
'That's what I'd do.'

'OK,' said Peter, 'I'm not buying.'

Tee hee.

Henry rolled. Six. Yes! He landed on
Eerie Eyrie. 'I'm buying it!' crowed Henry.

'But Henry,' said Peter, 'you just told
me not to buy it.'

'You shouldn't listen to me,' said Henry.

'MUM!' wailed Peter.

Soon Henry owned Eerie Eyrie,
Gryphon Gulch and Creepy Hollow,
but he was dangerously low on treasure.
Margaret owned Rocky Ravine,
Vulture Valley, and Hideous Hellmouth.
Margaret kept her treasure in her
treasure pouch, so it was impossible
to see how much money she had, but

Henry guessed she was also low.

Peter owned Demon Den and one dragon egg.

Margaret was stuck in the Dungeon. Yippee! This meant if Henry landed on one of her lairs he'd be safe. Horrid Henry rolled, and landed on Vulture Valley, guarded by a baby dragon.

'Gotcha!' shrieked Margaret. 'Gimme 25 rubies.'

'You're in the Dungeon, you can't collect ransom,' said Henry. 'Nah nah ne nah nah!'

'Can!'

'Can't!'

'That's how we play in *my* house,' said Margaret.

'In case you hadn't noticed, we're not *at* your house,' said Henry.

'But I'm the guest,' said Margaret. 'Gimme my money!'

'No!' shouted Henry. 'You can't just make up rules.'

'The rules say . . .' began Perfect Peter.

'Shut up, Peter!' screamed Henry and Margaret.

'I'm not paying,' said Henry.

Margaret glowered. 'I'll get you for this, Henry,' she hissed.

It was Peter's turn. Henry had just upgraded his baby dragon guarding Eerie Eyrie to a big, huge, fire-breathing, slavering monster dragon. Peter was only five squares away. If

Peter landed there, he'd be out of the game.

'Land! Land! Land! Land! Land!' chanted Henry. 'Yum yum yum, my dragon is just waiting to eat you up.'

'Stop it, Henry,' said Peter. He rolled. Five.

'Gotcha!' shouted Horrid Henry. 'I own Eerie Eyrie! You've landed in my lair, pay up! That's 100 rubies.'

'I don't have enough money,' wailed Perfect Peter.

Horrid Henry drew his finger

across his throat.

'You're dead meat, worm,' he chortled.

Perfect Peter burst into tears and ran out of the room.

'Waaaaaaahhhhh,' he wailed. 'I lost!'

Horrid Henry glared at Moody Margaret.

Moody Margaret glared at Horrid Henry.

'You're next to be eaten,' snarled Margaret.

'*You're* next,' snarled Henry.

Henry peeked under the *Gotcha* board where his treasure was hidden. Oh no. Not again. He'd spent so much on dragons he was down to his last few rubies. If he landed on any of Margaret's lairs, he'd be wiped out. He had to get more treasure. He had to. Why oh why had he let Margaret be banker?

His situation was desperate. Peter was easy to steal money from, but Margaret's eagle eyes never missed a trick. What to do, what to do? He had to get more treasure, he had to.

And then suddenly Horrid Henry had a brilliant, spectacular idea. It was so brilliant that Henry couldn't believe he'd never thought of it before. It was dangerous. It was risky. But what choice did he have?

'I need the loo,' said Henry.

'Hurry up,' said Margaret, scowling.

Horrid Henry dashed to the downstairs loo . . . and sneaked straight out of the back door. Then he jumped over the garden wall and crept into Margaret's house.

Quickly he ran to her sitting room

and scanned her games cupboard. Aha!
There was Margaret's *Gotcha*.

Horrid Henry stuffed his pockets with
treasure. He stuffed more under his shirt
and in his socks.

'Is that you, my little sugarplum?'
came a voice from upstairs. 'Maggie
Moo-Moo?'

Henry froze. Margaret's mum was
home.

'Maggie Plumpykins,' cooed her
mum, coming down the stairs. 'Is that
you–oooo?'

'No,' squeaked Henry. 'I mean,

yes,' he squawked. 'Got to go back to Henry's, 'bye!'

And Horrid Henry ran for his life.

'You took a long time,' said Margaret.

Henry hugged his stomach.

'Upset tummy,' he lied. Oh boy was he brilliant. Now, with loads of cash which he would slip under the board, he was sure to win.

Henry picked up the dice and handed them to Margaret.

'Your turn,' said Henry.

Henry's hungry dragon stood waiting six places away in Goblin Gorge.

Roll a six, roll a six, roll a six, prayed Horrid Henry.

Not a six, not a six, not a six, prayed Moody Margaret.

Margaret rolled. Four. She moved her skull to the Haunted Forest.

'Your turn,' said Margaret.

Henry rolled a three. Oh no. He'd landed on Hideous Hellmouth, where Margaret's giant dragon loomed.

'Yes!' squealed Margaret. 'Gotcha! You're dead! Ha ha hahaha, I won!' Moody Margaret leapt to her feet and did a victory dance, whooping and cheering.

Horrid Henry smiled at her.

'Oh dear,' said Horrid Henry. 'Oh dearie, dearie me. Looks like I'm dragon food — NOT!'

'What do you mean, not?' said

Margaret. 'You're dead meat, you can't pay me.'

'Not so fast,' said Horrid Henry. With a flourish he reached under the board and pulled out a wodge of treasure.

'Let me see, 100 rubies, is it?' said Henry, counting off a pile of coins.

Margaret's mouth dropped open.

'How did you . . . what . . . how . . . huh?' she spluttered.

Henry shrugged modestly. 'Some of us know how to play this game,' he said. 'Now roll.'

Moody Margaret rolled and landed on

a Fate square.

Go straight to Eerie Eyrie, read the card.

'Gotcha!' shrieked Horrid Henry. He'd won!! Margaret didn't have enough money to stop being eaten. She was dead. She was doomed.

'I won! I won! You can't pay me, nah nah ne nah nah,' shrieked Horrid Henry, leaping up and doing a victory dance. 'I am the *Gotcha* king!'

'Says who?' said Moody Margaret, pulling a handful of treasure from her pouch.

Huh?

'You stole that money!' spluttered Henry. 'You stole the bank's money. You big fat cheater.'

'Didn't.'

'Did.'

'CHEATER!' howled Moody Margaret.

'CHEATER!' howled Horrid Henry.

Moody Margaret grabbed the board and hurled it to the floor.

'I won,' said Horrid Henry.

'Did not.'

'Did too, Maggie Moo-Moo.'

'Don't call me that,' said Margaret, glaring.

'Call you what, Moo-Moo?'

'I challenge you to a re-match,' said Moody Margaret.

'You're on,' said Horrid Henry.

Henry's Holiday Howlers

What do elephants sing at Christmas?
No-elephants, No-elephants . . .

Knock, knock.
Who's there?
Rabbit.
Rabbit who?
Rabbit up neatly.
It's a Christmas present.

What's the best Christmas
present in the world?
A broken drum, you can't beat it!

What jumps out from behind a snowdrift
and shows you his bottom?
The A-bum-inable Snowman.

Who says "oh, oh, oh"?
Father Christmas walking backwards.

Why is a sofa like a
roast turkey?
Because it's full of
stuffing.

DAD: I'm trying to find a present
for my son. Can you help me out?
SHOP ASSISTANT: Certainly, sir.
Which way did you come in?

Why can't you tell
a joke while ice-
skating?
The ice might
crack up.

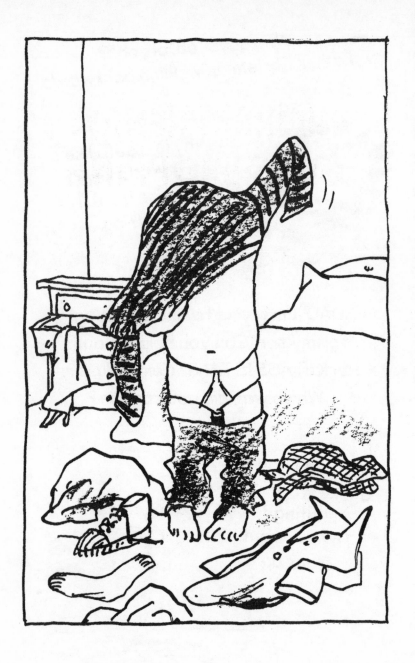

HORRID HENRY
GOES SHOPPING

Horrid Henry stood in his bedroom up to his knees in clothes. The long sleeve stripy T-shirt came to his elbow. His trousers stopped halfway down his legs. Henry sucked in his tummy as hard as he could. Still the zip wouldn't zip.

'Nothing fits!' he screamed, yanking off the shirt and hurling it across the room. 'And my shoes hurt.'

'All right Henry, calm down,' said Mum. 'You've grown. We'll go out this afternoon and get you some new clothes and shoes.'

'NOOOOOOO!' shrieked Henry. 'NOOOOOOOOOOOOO!'

Horrid Henry hated shopping.

Correction: Horrid Henry loved shopping. He loved shopping for gigantic TVs, computer games, comics, toys, and sweets. Yet for some reason Horrid Henry's parents never wanted to go shopping for good stuff. Oh no. They shopped for hoover bags. Toothpaste. Spinach. Socks. Why oh

74

why did he have such horrible parents?
When he was grown-up he'd never
set foot in a supermarket. He'd only
shop for TVs, computer games, and
chocolate.

But shopping for clothes was even
worse than heaving his heavy bones
round the Happy Shopper Supermarket.
Nothing was more boring than being
dragged round miles and miles and miles
of shops, filled with disgusting clothes
only a mutant would ever want to wear,
and then standing in a little room while
Mum made you try on icky scratchy
things you wouldn't be seen dead in
if they were the last trousers on earth.
It was horrible enough getting dressed
once a day without doing it fifty times.
Just thinking about trying on shirt after
shirt after shirt made Horrid Henry
want to scream.

75

'I'm not going shopping!' he howled,
kicking the pile of clothes as viciously as
he could. 'And you can't make me.'

'What's all this yelling?' demanded
Dad.

'Henry needs new trousers,' said Mum
grimly.

Dad went pale.

'Are you sure?'

'Yes,' said Mum. 'Take a look at him.'

Dad looked at Henry. Henry scowled.

'They're a *little* small, but not *that* bad,' said Dad.

'I can't breathe in these trousers!' shrieked Henry.

'That's why we're going shopping,' said Mum. 'And *I'll* take him.' Last time Dad had taken Henry shopping for socks and came back instead with three Hairy Hellhound CDs and a jumbo pack of Day–Glo slime.

'I don't know what came over me,' Dad had said, when Mum told him off.

'But why do *I* have to go?' said Henry. 'I don't want to waste my precious time shopping.'

'What about *my* precious time?' said Mum.

Henry scowled. Parents didn't have precious time. They were there to serve their children. New trousers should just magically appear, like clean clothes and packed lunches.

Mum's face brightened. 'Wait, I have an idea,' she beamed. She rushed out and came back with a large plastic bag. 'Here,' she said, pulling out a pair of bright red trousers, 'try these on.'

Henry looked at them suspiciously.

'Where are they from?'

'Aunt Ruby dropped off some of Steve's old clothes a few weeks ago. I'm sure we'll find something that fits you.'

Horrid Henry stared at Mum. Had she gone gaga? Was she actually suggesting that he should wear his horrible cousin's mouldy old shirts and pongy pants? Just imagine, putting his arms into the same stinky sleeves that Stuck-up Steve had slimed? Uggh!

'NO WAY!' screamed Henry, shuddering. 'I'm not wearing Steve's smelly old clothes. I'd catch rabies.'

'They're practically brand new,' said Mum.

'I don't care,' said Henry.

'But Henry,' said Perfect Peter. 'I always wear *your* hand-me-downs.'

'So?' snarled Henry.

'I don't mind wearing hand-me-downs,' said Perfect Peter. 'It saves so much money. You shouldn't be so selfish, Henry.'

'Quite right, Peter,' said Mum, smiling. 'At least *one* of my sons thinks about others.'

Horrid Henry pounced. He was a vampire sampling his supper.

'AAIIIEEEEEE!' squealed Peter.

'Stop that, Henry!' screamed Mum.

'Leave your brother alone!' screamed Dad.

Horrid Henry glared at Peter.

'Peter is a worm, Peter is a toad,' jeered Henry.

'Mum!' wailed Peter. 'Henry said I was a worm. And a toad.'

'Don't be horrid, Henry,' said Dad.
'Or no TV for a week. You have three
choices. Wear Steve's old clothes. Wear
your old clothes. Go shopping for new
ones today.'

'Do we *have* to go today?' moaned
Henry.

'Fine,' said Mum. 'We'll go
tomorrow.'

'I don't want to go tomorrow,'
wailed Henry. 'My weekend will be
ruined.'

Mum glared at Henry.

'Then we'll go right now this minute.'

NO!' screamed Horrid Henry.

'YES!' screamed Mum.

Several hours later, Mum and Henry
walked into Mellow Mall. Mum
already looked like she'd been crossing
the Sahara desert without water for

days. Serve
her right for
bringing me
here, thought
Horrid Henry,
scowling, as he
scuffed his feet.

'Can't we
go to Shop
'n' Drop?'
whined Henry.
'Graham says they've got a win your
weight in chocolate competition.'

'No,' said Mum, dragging Henry into
Zippy's Department Store. 'We're here
to get you some new trousers and shoes.
Now hurry up, we don't have all day.'

Horrid Henry looked around. Wow!
There was lots of great stuff on display.

'I want the Hip-Hop Robots,' said
Henry.

'No,' said Mum.

'I want the new Supersoaker!'
screeched Henry.

'No,' said Mum.

'I want a Creepy Crawly lunchbox!'

'NO!' said Mum, pulling him into the
boys' clothing department.

What, thought Horrid Henry grimly, is the point of going shopping if you never buy anything?

'I want Root-a-Toot trainers with flashing red lights,' said Henry. He could see himself now, strolling into class, a bugle blasting and red light flashing every time his feet hit the floor. Cool! He'd love to see Miss Battle-Axe's face when he exploded into class wearing them.

'No,' said Mum, shuddering.

'Oh please,' said Henry.

'NO!' said Mum, 'we're here to buy trousers and sensible school shoes.'

'But I want Root-a-Toot trainers!' screamed Horrid Henry. 'Why can't we buy what *I* want to buy? You're the meanest mother in the world and I hate you!'

'Don't be horrid, Henry. Go and try these on,' said Mum, grabbing a selection of hideous trousers and revolting T-shirts. 'I'll keep looking.'

Horrid Henry sighed loudly and slumped towards the dressing room. No one in the world suffered as much as he did. Maybe he could hide between the clothes racks and never come out.

Then something wonderful in the toy department next door caught his eye.

Whooa! A whole row of the new megalotronic animobotic robots with 213 programmable actions. Horrid Henry dumped the clothes and ran over to have a look. Oooh, the new Intergalactic Samurai Gorillas which launched real stinkbombs! And the latest Supersoakers! And deluxe Dungeon Drink kits with a celebrity chef recipe book! To say nothing of the Mega-Whirl Goo Shooter which sprayed fluorescent goo for fifty metres in every direction. Wow!

Mum staggered into the dressing room with more clothes. 'Henry?' said Mum.

No reply.

'HENRY!' said Mum.

Still no reply.

Mum yanked open a dressing room door.

'Hen—'

'Excuse *me*!' yelped a bald man, standing in his underpants.

'Sorry,' said Mum, blushing bright pink. She dashed out of the changing room and scanned the shop floor.

Henry was gone.

Mum searched up the aisles.

No Henry.

87

Mum searched down the aisles.

Still no Henry.

Then Mum saw a tuft of hair sticking up behind the neon sign for Ballistic Bazooka Boomerangs. She marched over and hauled Henry away.

'I was just looking,' protested Henry.

Henry tried on one pair of trousers after another.

'No, no, no, no, no, no, no,' said Henry, kicking off the final pair. 'I hate all of them.'

'All right,' said Mum, grimly. 'We'll look somewhere else.'

Mum and Henry went to Top Trousers.
They went to Cool Clothes. They went
to Stomp in the Swamp. Nothing had
been right.

'Too tight,' moaned Henry.

'Too itchy!'

'Too big!'

'Too small!'

'Too ugly!'

'Too red!'

'Too
uncomfortable!'

'We're going
to Tip-Top Togs,'
said Mum wearily.
'The first thing that fits,
we're buying.'

Mum staggered into the children's
department and grabbed a pair of pink
and green tartan trousers in Henry's
size.

'Try these on,' she ordered. 'If they fit we're having them.'

Horrid Henry gazed in horror at the horrendous trousers.

'Those are girls' trousers!' he screamed.

'They are not,' said Mum.

'Are too!' shrieked Henry.

'I'm sick and tired of your excuses, Henry,' said Mum. 'Put them on or no pocket money for a year. I mean it.'

Horrid Henry put on the pink and green tartan trousers, puffing out his stomach as much as possible. Not even Mum would make him buy trousers that were too tight.

Oh no. The horrible trousers had an elastic waist. They would fit a mouse as easily as an elephant.

'And lots of room to grow,' said Mum brightly. 'You can wear them for years. Perfect.'

'NOOOOOO!' howled Henry. He
flung himself on the floor kicking and
screaming. 'NOOOO! THEY'RE
GIRLS' TROUSERS!!!'

'We're buying them,' said Mum.
She gathered up the tartan trousers and
stomped over to the till. She tried not
to think about starting all over again
trying to find a pair of shoes that Henry
would wear.

A little girl in pigtails walked out of
the dressing room, twirling in pink and
green tartan trousers.

'I love them, Mummy!' she shrieked. 'Let's get three pairs.'

Horrid Henry stopped howling.

He looked at Mum.

Mum looked at Henry.

Then they both looked at the pink and green tartan trousers Mum was carrying.

ROOT-A-TOOT!
ROOT-A-TOOT!
ROOT-A-TOOT!
TOOT! TOOT!

An earsplitting bugle blast shook the house. Flashing red lights bounced off the walls.

'What's that noise?' said Dad, covering his ears.

'What noise?' said Mum, pretending to read.

ROOT-A-TOOT!
ROOT-A-TOOT!
ROOT-A-TOOT!
TOOT! TOOT!

Dad stared at Mum.

'You didn't,' said Dad. 'Not—Root-a-Toot trainers?'

Mum hid her face in her hands.

'I don't know what came over me,' said Mum.

Henry's Holiday Howlers

What do you call a reindeer who won't say please and thank you?
Rude-olph.

What's the most musical part of a turkey?
The drumstick.

What's the wettest animal in the world?
Rain-deer.

MUM: Did you like the dictionary I gave you for Christmas?
PERFECT PETER: Yes, I've been trying to find the words to thank you.

Knock, knock.
Who's there?
Chile.
Chile who?
Chile being an
abominable snowman.

Did you hear about the wolves'
Christmas party?
It was a howling success.

What did the bald man say when
he got a comb for Christmas?
Thanks, I'll never part with it.

How do monsters cook their Christmas lunch?
They terror-fry it.

HORRID HENRY'S INVASION

'Baa! Baa! Baa!'

Perfect Peter baaed happily at his sheep collection. There they were, his ten lovely little sheepies, all beautifully lined up from biggest to smallest, heads facing forward, fluffy tails against the wall, all five centimetres apart from one another, all—

Perfect Peter gasped. Something was wrong. Something was terribly wrong. But what? What? Peter scanned the mantelpiece. Then he saw . . .

Nooooo!

Fluff Puff, his favourite sheep, the one with the pink and yellow nose, was facing the wrong way round. His nose was shoved against the wall. His tail was facing forward. And he was . . . he was . . . crooked!

This could only mean . . . this could only mean . . .

'Mum!' screamed Peter. 'Mum! Henry's been in my room again!'

'Henry!' shouted Mum. 'Keep out of Peter's room.'

'I'm not in Peter's room,' yelled Horrid Henry. 'I'm in mine.'

'But he was,' wailed Peter.

'Wasn't!' bellowed Horrid Henry.

Tee hee.

Horrid Henry was strictly forbidden to go into Peter's bedroom without Peter's permission. But sometimes, thought

Horrid Henry, when Peter was being even more of a toady toad than usual, he had no choice but to invade.

Peter had run blabbing to Mum that Henry had watched *Mutant Max* and *Knight Fight* when Mum had said he could only watch one or the other. Henry had been banned from watching TV all day. Peter was such a telltale frogface ninnyhammer toady poo bag, thought Horrid Henry grimly. Well, just wait till Peter tried to colour in his new picture, he'd—

'MUM!' screamed Peter. 'Henry switched the caps on my coloured pens. I just put pink in the sky.'

'Didn't!' yelled Henry.

'Did!' wailed Peter.

'Prove it,' said Horrid Henry, smirking.

Mum came upstairs. Quickly Henry leapt over the mess covering the floor of his room, flopped on his bed and grabbed a *Screamin' Demon* comic. Peter came and stood in the doorway.

'Henry's being horrid,' snivelled Peter.

'Henry, have you been in Peter's room?' said Mum.

Henry sighed loudly. 'Of course I've been in his smelly room. I live here, don't I?'

'I mean when he wasn't there,' said Mum.

'No,' said Horrid Henry. This wasn't a lie, because even if Peter *wasn't* there his horrible stinky smell was.

'He has too,' said Peter. 'Fluff Puff was turned the wrong way round.'

'Maybe he was just trying to escape from your pongy pants,' said Henry. '*I* would.'

'Mum!' said Peter.

'Henry! Don't be horrid. Leave your brother alone.'

'I *am* leaving him alone,' said Horrid Henry. 'Why can't he leave *me* alone? And get out of *my* room, Peter!' he shrieked, as Peter put his foot just inside Henry's door.

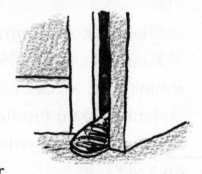

Peter quickly withdrew his foot.

Henry glared at Peter.

Peter glared at Henry.

Mum sighed. 'The next one who goes into the other's room without permission will be banned from the computer for a week. And no pocket money either.'

She turned to go.

Henry stuck out his tongue at Peter.

'Telltale,' he mouthed.

'Mum!' screamed Peter.

Perfect Peter stalked back to his bedroom. How dare Henry sneak in and mess up his sheep? What a mean, horrible brother. Perhaps he needed to calm down and listen to a little music. The *Daffy and her Dancing Daisies Greatest Hits* CD always cheered him up.

'Dance and prance. Prance and dance.
You say moo moo. We say baa.
Everybody says moo moo baa baa,'
piped Perfect Peter as he put on the
Daffy CD.

**Boils on your fat face
Boils make you dumb.
Chop Chop Chop 'em off
Stick 'em on your bum!**

blared the CD player.

Huh? What was that horrible song?
Peter yanked out the CD. It was the
Skullbangers singing the horrible 'Bony
Boil' song. Henry must have sneaked a
Skullbanger CD inside the Daffy case.
How dare he? How dare he? Peter
would storm straight downstairs and
tell Mum. Henry would get into big
trouble. Big big trouble.

Then Peter paused. There *was* the
teeny-tiny possibility that Peter had

mixed them up by mistake . . . No.
He needed absolute proof of Henry's
horridness. He'd do his homework, then
have a good look around Henry's room
to see if his Daffy CD was hidden there.

Peter glanced at his 'To Do' list
pinned on his noticeboard. When he'd
written it that morning it read:

Peter's To Do List
Practise cello
Fold clothes and put away
Do homework
Brush my teeth
Read Bunny's Big Boo Boo

The list now read:

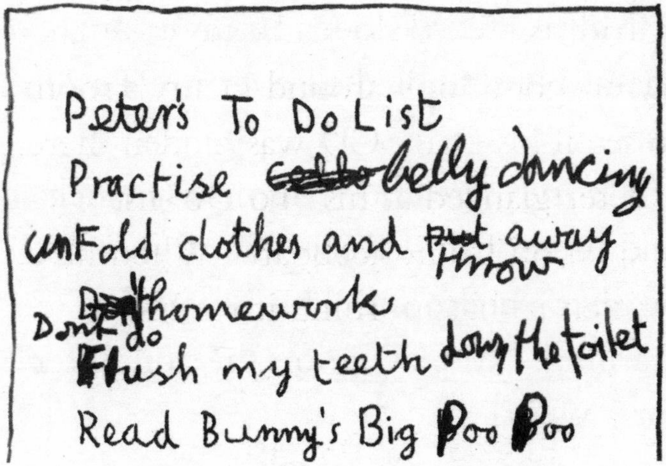

Peter's To Do List
Practise ~~cello~~ belly dancing
unFold clothes and ~~Put~~ away throw
~~Do~~ my homework Don't do
~~Flush~~ my teeth down the toilet
Read Bunny's Big ~~Poo~~ Poo

At the bottom someone had added:

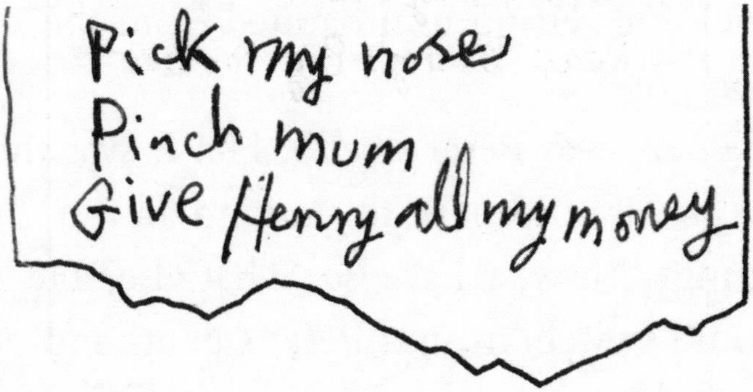

Pick my nose
Pinch mum
Give Henry all my money

Well, here was proof! He was going to go straight down and tell on Henry.

'Mum! Henry's been in my room again. He scribbled all over my To Do list.'

'Henry!' screamed Mum. 'I am sick and tired of this! Keep out of your brother's bedroom! This is your last warning! No playing on the computer for a week!'

Sneak. Sneak. Sneak.

Horrid Henry slipped inside the enemy's bedroom. He'd pay Peter back for getting him banned from the computer.

There was Peter's cello. Ha! It was the work of a moment to unwind all the strings. Now, what else, what else? He could switch around Peter's pants and sock drawers.

No! Even better. Quickly Henry undid all of Peter's socks, and mismatched them. Who said socks should match?

Tee hee. Peter would go mad when he found out he was wearing one Sammy the Snail sock with one Daffy sock. Then Henry snatched Bunnykins off Peter's bed and crept out.

Sneak. Sneak. Sneak.

Perfect Peter crept down the hall and stood outside Henry's bedroom, holding a muddy twig. His heart was pounding. Peter knew he was strictly forbidden to go into Henry's room without permission. But Henry kept breaking that rule. So why shouldn't he?

Squaring his shoulders, Peter tiptoed in.

Crunch.

Crunch.

Crunch.

Henry's room was a pigsty, thought Perfect Peter, wading through broken knights, crumpled sweet wrappers, dirty clothes, ripped comics, and muddy shoes.

Mr Kill. He'd steal Mr Kill. Ha! Serve Henry right. And he'd put the muddy twig in Henry's bed. Serve him double right. Perfect Peter grabbed Mr Kill, shoved the twig in Henry's bed and nipped back to his room.

And screamed.

Fluff Puff wasn't just turned the wrong way, he was – gone! Henry must have stolen him. And Lambykins was gone

too. And Squish. Peter only had seven
sheep left. 🐑 🐑 🐑 🐑 🐑 🐑 🐑

And where was his Bunnykins? He
wasn't on the bed where he belonged.
No!!!!!! This was the last straw. This
was war.

The coast was clear. Peter always took
ages having his bath. Horrid Henry
slipped into the worm's room.

He'd pay Peter back for stealing Mr

Kill. There he was, shoved at the top of
Peter's wardrobe, where Peter always
hid things he didn't want Henry to find.
Well, ha ha ha, thought Horrid Henry,
rescuing Mr Kill.

Now what to do, what to do?
Horrid Henry scooped up all of Peter's
remaining sheep and shoved them inside
Peter's pillowcase.

What else? Henry glanced round
Peter's immaculate room. He could
mess it up. Nah, thought Henry.
Peter loved tidying. He could – aha.

Peter had pinned drawings all over
the wall above his bed. Henry surveyed
them. Shame, thought Henry, that
Peter's pictures were all so dull. I
mean, really, 'My Family', and
'My Bunnykins'. Horrid Henry
climbed on Peter's bed to reach the
drawings.

Poor Peter, thought Horrid Henry.
What a terrible artist he was. No
wonder he was such a smelly toad if he
had to look at such awful pictures all
the time. Perhaps Henry could improve
them . . .

Now, let's see, thought Horrid Henry,
getting out some crayons. Drawing
a crown on my head would be a big

improvement. There! That livens things up. And a big red nose on Peter would help, too, thought Henry, drawing away. So would a droopy moustache on Mum. And as for that stupid picture of Bunnykins, well, why not draw a lovely toilet for him to—

'What are you doing in here?' came a little voice.

Horrid Henry turned.

There was Peter, in his bunny pyjamas, glaring at him.

Uh oh. If Peter told on him again, Henry would be in big, big, mega-big trouble. Mum would probably ban him from the computer for ever.

'You're in my room. I'm telling on you,' shrieked Peter.

'Shhh!' hissed Horrid Henry.

'What do you mean, shhh?' said Peter. 'I'm going straight down to tell Mum.'

'One word and you're dead, worm,' said Horrid Henry. 'Quick! Close the door.'

Perfect Peter looked behind him.

'Why?'

'Just do it, worm,' hissed Henry.

Perfect Peter shut the door.

'What are you doing?' he demanded.

'Dusting for fingerprints,' said Horrid Henry smoothly.

Fingerprints?

'What?' said Peter.

'I thought I heard someone in your room, and ran in to check you were okay. Just look what I found,' said Horrid Henry dramatically, pointing to Peter's now empty mantelpiece.

Peter let out a squeal.

'My sheepies!' wailed Peter.

'I think there's a burglar in the house,' whispered Horrid Henry

urgently. 'And I think he's hiding . . . in your room.'

Peter gulped. A burglar? In his room?

'A burglar?'

'Too right,' said Henry. 'Who do you think stole Bunnykins? And all your sheep?'

'You,' said Peter.

Horrid Henry snorted. 'No! What would I want with your stupid sheep? But a sheep rustler would love them.'

Perfect Peter hesitated. Could Henry
be telling the truth? *Could* a burglar
really have stolen his sheep?

'I think he's hiding under the bed,'
hissed Horrid Henry. 'Why don't you
check?'

Peter stepped back.

'No,' said Peter. 'I'm scared.'

'Then get out of here as quick as you
can,' whispered Henry. '*I'll* check.'

'Thank you, Henry,' said Peter.

Perfect Peter crept into the hallway. Then he stopped. Something wasn't right . . . something was a little bit wrong.

Perfect Peter marched back into his bedroom. Henry was by the door.

'I think the burglar is hiding in your wardrobe, I'll get—'

'You said you were fingerprinting,' said Peter suspiciously. 'With what?'

'My fingers,' said Horrid Henry. 'Why do you think it's called *finger*printing?'

Then Peter caught sight of his drawings.

'You've ruined my pictures!' shrieked Peter.

'It wasn't me, it must have been the burglar,' said Horrid Henry.

'You're trying to trick me,' said Peter. 'I'm telling!'

Time for Plan B.

'I'm only in here 'cause you were in my room,' said Henry.

'Wasn't!'

'Were!'

'Liar!'

117

'Liar!'

'You stole Bunnykins!'

'You stole Mr Kill!'

'Thief!'

'Thief!'

'I'm telling on you.'

'I'm telling on you!'

Henry and Peter glared at each other.

'Okay,' said Horrid Henry. 'I won't invade your room if you won't invade mine.'

'Okay,' said Perfect Peter. He'd agree to anything to get Henry to leave his sheep alone.

Horrid Henry smirked.

He couldn't wait until tomorrow when Peter tried to play his cello . . . tee hee.

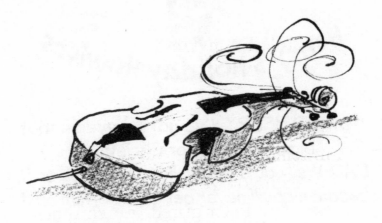

Wouldn't he get a shock!

Henry's Holiday Howlers

HORRID HENRY: I've got my eye on that big shiny bike for Christmas.
DAD: Well you'd better keep your eye on it, because you'll never get your bottom on it.

Who gives presents to children, then gobbles them up?
Santa Jaws.

Why do reindeer scratch themselves?
Because no one knows where they itch.

Knock, knock.
Who's there?
Wayne.
Wayne who?
(Sing) "Wayne in a manger, no crib for a bed."

What does a cat on the beach have in common with Christmas?
Sandy Claws.

Why does Father Christmas go down the chimney?
Because it soots him.

What do you get if you cross a goldfish and an ice cube?
A cold fish.

HENRY: Where do fleas go in winter?
FLUFFY: Search me.

HORRiD HENRY'S HORRiD WEEKEND

'NOOOOOOOOO!' screamed Horrid Henry. 'I don't want to spend the weekend with Steve.'

'Don't be horrid, Henry,' said Mum. 'It's very kind of Aunt Ruby to invite us down for the weekend.'

'But I hate Aunt Ruby!' shrieked Henry. 'And I hate Steve and I hate you!'

'I can't wait to go,' said Perfect Peter.

'Shut up, Peter!' howled Henry.

'Don't tell your brother to shut up,' shouted Mum.

'Shut up! Shut up! Shut up!' And Horrid Henry fell to the floor wailing and screaming and kicking.

Stuck-Up Steve was Horrid Henry's hideous cousin. Steve hated Henry. Henry hated him. The last time Henry had seen Steve, Henry had tricked him into thinking there was a monster under his bed. Steve had sworn revenge. Then there was the other time at the restaurant when . . . well, Horrid Henry thought it would be a good idea to avoid Steve until his cousin was grown-up and in prison for crimes against humanity.

And now his mean, horrible parents were forcing him to spend a whole precious weekend with the toadiest, wormiest, smelliest boy who ever slimed out of a swamp.

Mum sighed. 'We're going and that's that. Ruby says Steve is having a lovely friend over so that should be extra fun.'

Henry stopped screaming and kicking. Maybe Steve's friend wouldn't be a stuck-up monster. Maybe *he'd* been forced to waste his weekend with Steve, too. After all, who'd volunteer to spend time with Steve? Maybe together they could squish Stuck-Up Steve once and for all.

Ding dong.

Horrid Henry, Perfect Peter, Mum and Dad stood outside Rich Aunt Ruby's enormous house on a grey, drizzly day.

Steve opened the massive front door.

'Oh,' he sneered. 'It's you.'

Steve opened the present Mum had brought. It was a small flashlight. Steve put it down.

'I already have a much better one,' he said.

'Oh,' said Mum.

Another boy stood beside him. A boy who looked vaguely familiar. A boy . . . Horrid Henry gasped. Oh no. It was Bill. Bossy Bill. The horrible son of Dad's boss. Henry had once tricked Bill into photocopying his bottom. Bill had sworn revenge. Horrid Henry's insides turned to jelly. Trust Stuck-Up Steve to be friends with Bossy Bill. It was bad enough being trapped in a house with one Arch-Enemy. Now he was stuck in a house with TWO . . .

Stuck-up Steve scowled at Henry.
'You're wearing that old shirt of mine,'
he said. 'Don't your parents ever buy
you new clothes?'

Bossy Bill snorted.

'Steve,' said Aunt Ruby. 'Don't be
rude.'

'I wasn't,' said Steve. 'I was just asking.
No harm in asking, is there?'

'No,' said Horrid Henry. He smiled
at Steve. 'So when will Aunt Ruby buy
you a new face?'

'Henry,' said Mum. 'Don't be rude.'

'I was just asking,' said Henry. 'No harm in asking, is there?' he added, glaring at Steve.

Steve glared back.

Aunt Ruby beamed. 'Henry, Steve and Bill are taking you to their friend Tim's paintballing party.'

'Won't that be fun,' said Mum.

Peter looked frightened.

'Don't worry, Peter,' said Aunt Ruby, 'you can help me plant seedlings while the older boys are out.'

Peter beamed. 'Thank you,' he said. 'I don't like paintballing. Too messy and scary.'

Paintballing! Horrid Henry loved paintballing. The chance to splat Steve and Bill with ooey gooey globs of paint . . . hmmm, maybe the weekend was looking up.

'Great!' said Horrid Henry.

'How nice,' said Rich Aunt Ruby,
'you boys already know each other.
Think how much fun you're all going to
have sharing Steve's bedroom together.'

Uh-oh, thought Horrid Henry.

'Yeah!' said Stuck-Up Steve. 'We're
looking forward to sharing a room with
Henry.' His piggy eyes gleamed.

'Yeah!' said Bossy Bill. 'I can't wait.'
His piggy eyes gleamed.

'Yeah,' said Horrid Henry. He wouldn't be sleeping a wink.

Horrid Henry looked around the enormous high-ceilinged bedroom he'd be sharing with his two evil enemies for two very long days and one very long night. There was a bunk-bed, which Steve and Bill had already nabbed, and two single beds. Steve's bedroom shelves were stuffed with zillions of new toys and games, as usual.

Bill and Steve smirked at each other. Henry scowled at them. What were they plotting?

'Don't you dare touch my Super-Blooper Blaster,' said Steve.

'Don't you dare touch my Demon Dagger Sabre,' said Bill.

A Super-Blooper Blaster! A Demon Dagger Sabre! Trust Bill and Steve to

have the two best toys in the world . . .
Rats.

'Don't worry,' said Henry. 'I don't
play with baby toys.'

'Oh yeah,' said Stuck-Up Steve. 'Bet
you're too much of a baby to jump off
my top bunk onto your bed.'

'Am not,' said Henry.

'We're not allowed to jump on beds,'
said Perfect Peter.

'We're not allowed,' mimicked Steve.
'I thought you were too poor to even
have beds.'

'Ha ha,' said Henry.

'Chicken. Chicken. Scaredy cat,'
sneered Bossy Bill.

'Squawk!' said Stuck-Up Steve. 'I
knew you'd be too scared, chicken.'

That did it. *No* one called Horrid
Henry chicken and lived. As if he,
Henry, leader of a pirate gang, would be

afraid to jump off a top bunk. Ha.

'Don't do it, Henry,' said Perfect
Peter.

'Shut up, worm,' said Henry.

'But it's so high,' squealed Peter,
squeezing his eyes shut.

Horrid Henry clambered up the ladder and stepped onto the top bunk. 'It's nothing,' he lied. 'I've jumped off MUCH higher.'

'Well, go on then,' said Stuck-Up Steve.

Boing! Horrid Henry bounced.

Boing! Horrid Henry bounced higher. Whee! This bed was very springy.

'We're waiting, chicken,' said Bossy Bill.

BOING! BOING! Horrid Henry bent his knees, then – – – leap! He jumped onto the single bed below.

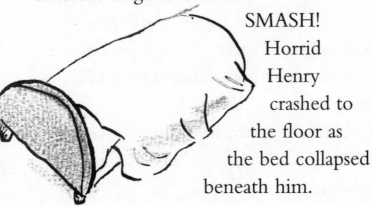

SMASH! Horrid Henry crashed to the floor as the bed collapsed beneath him.

Huh? What? How could he have broken the bed? He hadn't heard any breaking sounds.

It was as if . . . as if . . .

Mum, Dad and Aunt Ruby ran into the room.

'Henry broke the bed,' said Stuck-Up Steve.

'We tried to stop him,' said Bossy Bill, 'but Henry insisted on jumping.'

'But . . . but . . .' said Horrid Henry.

'Henry!' wailed Mum. 'You horrid boy.'

'How could you be so horrid?' said Dad. 'No pocket money for a year. Ruby, I'm so sorry.'

Aunt Ruby pursed her lips. 'These things happen,' she said.

'And no paintballing party for you,' said Mum.

What?

'No!' wailed Henry.

Then Horrid Henry saw a horrible sight. Behind Aunt Ruby's back, Steve and Bill were covering their mouths and laughing. Henry realised the terrible truth. Bill and Steve had tricked him.

They'd broken the bed. And now *he'd* got the blame.

'But I didn't break it!' screamed Henry.

'Yes you did, Henry,' said Peter. 'I saw you.'

AAAARRRRGGGGHHHH! Horrid Henry leapt at Peter. He was a storm god hurling thunderbolts at a foolish mortal.

'AAAIIIEEEEEE!' squealed Perfect Peter.

'Henry! Stop it!' shrieked Mum. 'Leave your brother alone.'

Nah nah ne nah nah mouthed Steve behind Aunt Ruby's back.

'Isn't it lovely how nicely the boys are playing together?' said Aunt Ruby.

'Yes, isn't it?' said Mum.

'Not surprising,' said Aunt Ruby, beaming. 'After all, Steve is such a polite, friendly boy, I've never met anyone who didn't love him.'

Snore! Snore! Snore!

Horrid Henry lay on a mattress listening to hideous snoring sounds. He'd stayed awake for hours, just in case they tried anything horrible, like pouring

water on his head, or stuffing frogs in his
bed. Which was what he was going to
do to Peter, the moment he got home.

Henry had just spent the most horrible
Saturday of his life. He'd begged to go to
the paintballing party. He'd pleaded to go
to the paintballing party. He'd screamed
about going to the paintballing party. But
no. His mean, horrible parents wouldn't
budge. And it was all Steve and Bill's fault.
They'd tripped him going down the stairs.

They'd kicked him under the table at
dinner (and then complained that he
was kicking *them*). And every time Aunt
Ruby's back was turned they stuck out
their tongues and jeered: 'We're going
paintballing, and you're not.'

He had to get to that party. And he
had to be revenged. But how? How? His
two Arch-Enemies had banded together
and struck the first blow.

Could he booby-trap their beds and
remove a few slats? Unfortunately,
everyone would know *he'd* done it
and he'd be in even more trouble
than he was now.

Scare them? Tell them there was a
monster under the bed? Hmmm. He
knew Steve was as big a scaredy cat
as Peter. But he'd already done that
once. He didn't think Steve would
fall for it again.

Get them into trouble? Turn them against each other? Steal their best toys and hide them? Hmmm. Hmmm. Horrid Henry thought and thought. He had to be revenged. He had to.

Tweet tweet. It was Sunday morning. The birds were singing. The sun was shining. The—

Yank!

Bossy Bill and Stuck-Up Steve pulled off his duvet.

'Nah na ne nah nah, we-ee beat you,' crowed Bill.

'Nah na ne nah nah, we got you into trouble,' crowed Steve.

Horrid Henry scowled. Time to put Operation Revenge into action.

'Bill thinks you're bossy, Steve,' said Henry. 'He told me.'

'Didn't,' said Bossy Bill.

'And Steve thinks you're stuck-up, Bill,' added Henry sweetly.

'No I don't,' said Steve.

'Then why'd you tell me that?' said Horrid Henry.

Steve stuck his nose in the air. 'Nice try Henry, you big loser,' said Stuck-Up Steve. 'Just ignore him, Bill.'

'Henry, it's not nice to tell lies,' said Perfect Peter.

'Shut up, worm,' snarled Horrid Henry.

Rats.

Time for plan B.

Except he didn't have a plan B.

'I can't wait for Tim's party,' said Bossy Bill. 'You never know what's going to happen.'

'Yeah, remember when he told us he was having a pirate party and instead we went to the Wild West Theme Park!' said Steve.

'Or when he said we were having a sleepover, and instead we all went to a Manic Buzzards concert.'

'And Tim gives the best party bags. Last year everyone got a Deluxe Demon Dagger Sabre,' said Steve. 'Wonder what he'll give this year? Oh, I forgot, Henry won't be coming to the party.'

'Too bad you can't come, Henry,' sneered Bossy Bill.

'Yeah, too bad,' sneered Stuck-Up Steve. 'Not.'

ARRRRGGGHH. Horrid Henry's blood boiled. He couldn't decide what was worse, listening to them crow about having got him into so much trouble, or brag about the great party they were going to and he wasn't.

'I can't wait to find out what surprises he'll have in store this year,' said Bill.

'Yeah,' said Steve.

Who cares? thought Horrid Henry.
Unless Tim was planning to throw Bill
and Steve into a shark tank. That would
be a nice surprise. Unless of course . . .

And then suddenly Horrid Henry had a brilliant, spectacular idea. It was so brilliant, and so spectacular, that for a moment he wondered whether he could stop himself from flinging open the window and shouting his plan out loud. Oh wow. Oh wow. It was risky. It was dangerous. But if it worked, he would have the best revenge ever in the history of the world. No, the history of the solar system. No, the history of the universe!

It was an hour before the party. Horrid Henry was counting the seconds until he could escape.

Aunt Ruby popped her head round the door waving an envelope.

'Letter for you boys,' she said.

Steve snatched it and tore it open.

143

Dear Steve and Bill
Party of the year update.
Everyone must come to my house
wearing pyjamas (you'll find
out why later, but don't be
surprised if we all end up in
a film — shhhh). It'll be a real
laugh. Make sure to bring
your favourite soft toys, too,
and wear your fluffiest
slippers. Hollywood, here
we come!

Tim

'He must be planning something
amazing,' said Bill.

'I bet we're all going to be acting in a

film!' said Steve.

'Yeah!' said Bill.

'Too bad *you* won't, Henry,' said Stuck-Up Steve.

'You're so lucky,' said Henry. 'I wish I were going.'

Mum looked at Dad.

Dad looked at Mum.

Henry held his breath.

'Well, you can't, Henry, and that's final,' said Mum.

'It's so unfair!' shrieked Henry.

Henry's parents dropped Steve and Bill off at Tim's party on their way home. Steve was in his blue bunny pyjamas and blue bunny fluffy slippers, and clutching a panda.

Bill was in his yellow duckling pyjamas and yellow duckling fluffy slippers, and clutching his monkey.

145

'Shame you can't come, Henry,' said Steve, smirking. 'But we'll be sure to tell you all about it.'

'Do,' said Henry, as Mum drove off.

Horrid Henry heard squeals of laughter at Hoity-Toity Tim's front door. Bill and Steve stood frozen. Then they started to wave frantically at the car.

'Are they saying something?' said Mum, glancing in the rear-view mirror.

'Nah, just waving goodbye,' said Horrid Henry. He rolled down his window.

'Have fun, guys!'

Henry's Holiday Howlers

Why did the snowman
send his father to
Siberia?
Because he wanted
frozen pop.

What do they sing in the desert
at Christmas time?
"Oh camel ye faithful..."

What do you get when
you cross a pirate
with Santa Claus?
Yo ho ho ho!

PATIENT: Doctor, doctor, I keep thinking
I'm a snowman.
DOCTOR: Keep cool.

What did the executioner say to his mother? *Only thirty chopping days to Christmas.*

Why do birds fly south for winter? *Because it's too far to walk.*

How do sheep keep warm in the winter? *They turn on the central bleating.*

What kind of money do snowmen use? *Ice lolly.*

HORRiD HENRY'S
FESTiVE
FUN

SEASONAL SPLITS

Below are eight festive six-letter words,
but they've all been split in half.
Can you solve the Christmassy clues
and put the pairs together?

KEY	TUR	SLE	ANG
TIN	IGH	CLE	GLO
ELS	CAR	SEL	ICI
JUM	VES	OLS	PER

This tastes yummy with gravy and stuffing	**TUR**	**KEY**
People come to your door and sing these		
There are usually lots of these in the school nativity		
Father Christmas travels on one of these		
This can be used to decorate your tree		
This forms when it's very cold		
You'll need to wear these when you go outside		
Henry thinks this is one of the worst gifts EVER!		

HORRiD HENRY'S LETTER

My mean old parents always give me horrible presents, so I've got to make absolutely sure that Father Christmas gives me what I want. I can't leave anything to chance. It's time to get writing . . .

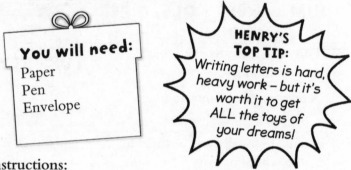

You will need:
Paper
Pen
Envelope

HENRY'S TOP TIP: Writing letters is hard, heavy work – but it's worth it to get ALL the toys of your dreams!

Instructions:

1. Grab a pen and paper and start your letter with: 'Dear Father Christmas'. He'll like that.

2. Write a list of all the toys you want. Father Christmas is getting old and needs a lot of help.

3. Make sure he knows what you don't want too – bleucch!

4. Fold up your letter and pop it in the envelope. Write 'Father Christmas' on the front and give it to your parents to post

5. Have a rest – you deserve it.

Dear Father Christmas
I want loads and loads of cash,
to make up for the puny ammount you
put in my stocking last year. And a
Robomatic Supersonic Space Howler Deluxe
plus attachments would be great, too.
I have asked for this before, you know!
And the Terminator Gladiator fighting
kit. I need lots more Day-Glo slime
and comics and a Mutant Max
poster and the new Zapatron HipHop
Dinosaur. This is your last chance.

Henry

P.S. Satzumas are NOT presents!!!

P.P.S Peter asked me to tell you to
     give me all his presents as
     he doesn't want any.

155

GREEDY GRAHAM'S ADVENT CALENDAR

Greedy Graham counts down to Christmas
with a sweet covered tree.

You will need:
A large piece of stiff cardboard
Pencils, paints and felt tip pens
Double-sided sticky tape
Silver foil or coloured tissue
  paper
Scissors
24 sweets or chocolates
24 sticky dots

GREEDY GRAHAM'S TIP:
Make the calendar as big as you can, so there's room for 24 REALLY BIG sweets!

Instructions:

1. Draw a big Christmas tree on the piece of cardboard and paint or colour it green. Carefully cut out your tree.

2. Wrap up 24 of your favourite sweets, chocolates (or another treat) in silver foil or coloured tissue paper.

3. Fasten the sweets to your Christmas tree picture with double-sided sticky tape.

4. Write numbers 1–24 on the sticky dots.

5. Stick one dot on each sweet in any order.

6. Enjoy a sweet every day from 1st December until Christmas Eve!

HORRID HENRY'S COUNTDOWN TO CHRISTMAS

Wednesday 1: Hooray! I can start opening my advent calendar. Aaaagh! There aren't any chocolates – just stupid boring pictures.

Thursday 2: I've started my letter to Father Christmas extra early – to make double sure he knows what I want. Remember, Father Christmas, satsumas are NOT presents.

Friday 3: Miss Battle-Axe has chosen the parts for the Christmas Nativity. Peter's Joseph and I'm the innkeeper, but I've only got one line. It's not fair! I should be the star of the show, not my stupid worm of a brother.

Saturday 4: Mum and Dad are so busy writing their Christmas cards, I get to watch TV all day. Tee hee!

Sunday 5: Mum drags me out on a walk in the countryside to pick holly for decorations. This is the worst day of my life.

Monday 6: I've sneaked a bit of Mum's holly and put it on Miss Battle-Axe's chair. Tee hee!

Tuesday 7: We're making Christmas baubles at school. I'm going to throw mine at Peter on the way home!

Wednesday 8: We're rehearsing for the nativity. Miss Battle-Axe won't let me improve my part with a dance.

Thursday 9: I've found the secret Christmas Day sweet stash!

Friday 10: It's snowing!

Saturday 11: I bombed Peter with snowballs, but he cried, and Dad told me not to be horrid. Peter's a crybaby poopy pants!

Sunday 12: Mum and Dad are baking horrible Christmassy food.

Monday 13: More rehearsals at school. Miss Battle-Axe won't let me add even a teeny-weeny-little song to my part.

Tuesday 14: I'm making the perfect present for Peter. A stinkbomb!

Wednesday 15: It's the school Christmas Fair – I've won a box of chocolates. Mum tells me I've got to give them to Granny.

Thursday 16: I've scoffed the chocolates. I won them – not Granny!

Friday 17: Mum and Dad are going Christmas shopping tomorrow, so I'm being extra nice to them. I even ate my vegetables at teatime.

Saturday 18: I had to trail around the shops with my family, and they didn't even buy me one tiny present. It's not fair! I ate loads of slimy vegetables for nothing.

Sunday 19: Peter is scratching out carols on his cello and Mum and Dad are singing. I'm playing the Smelly Bellies VERY loudly.

Monday 20: It's showtime! The nativity goes wrong – but I save the show. A star is born!

Tuesday 21: Last day of school. Hooray!

Wednesday 22: It's the holidays. I can watch TV for two weeks. Knight Fight – yeah!

Thursday 23: Oh no! I haven't got any presents for anybody. I write some nice Christmassy poems instead. Not bad, and cheap too!

Friday 24: I want Terminator Gladiator on the top of the Christmas tree. It looks much better than the stupid fairy that we always have.

Saturday 25: It's four o'clock on Christmas morning. I've opened all my presents and have chucked all my satsumas, socks and handkerchiefs in the bin where they belong. But Father Christmas wasn't completely useless this year – he got me a brilliant water pistol, so I'm having loads of fun spraying everyone. Mum and Dad don't look very pleased!

Happy Christmas!

CRAZY CHRISTMAS LUNCH

Christmas is all about stuffing your face with lots of yummy food. But did you know these crazy facts about Christmas lunch?

☆ At Christmas, people in the UK eat **19,000** tons of turkey, **120,000** tons of potatoes, **1,200** tons of parsnips, **1,600** tons of chestnuts, **7.5 million** carrots, **16 million** packets of stuffing, **11 million** Christmas cakes, and **40,000** tons of clementines, mandarins and satsumas.

☆ Sprouts were first eaten at Christmas in the **sixteenth century** – and they've been popular ever since!

☆ **175 million** mince pies are eaten in the UK over Christmas. If these were stacked on top of each other, they would stretch **3,262 miles** high – that's nearly **600 times** the height of Mount Everest!

☆ Mince pies get their name from their original filling which contained **minced meat** as well as fruits and spices.

☆ Not everyone eats turkey for Christmas dinner. In Denmark, it's traditional to eat **goose**, in Greece they eat **lamb**, and in Hungary, they eat **spicy chicken**.

☆ In New Zealand and Australia, it's **hot** in December, and Christmas lunch can be a **picnic** on the beach.

CHRISTMAS CONCERT CRISS-CROSS

Horrid Henry and his classmates
put together a band to entertain the school
at the Christmas concert. Can you answer
the clues from the pictures below and
fill in the crossword?

CLUES

Down

1. What brass instrument is
   Moody Margaret playing?
3. What is Soraya doing?
4. Perfect Peter is playing which string
   instrument?

Across

2. What is Horrid Henry playing?
5. What woodwind instrument is
   Weepy William playing?

HORRiD HENRY'S MONEY-MAKiNG MASTERCLASS

Spent all of your pocket money on comics and sweets like Henry? Here are a few of his top tips for making some cash when you need to buy last-minute Christmas presents . . .

☆ Set up a stall and sell all of your old baby toys at top prices. Help yourself to your wormy worm brother's good toys. He's got far too many.

☆ Tell your parents that you're going to be perfect for a whole day – but only if they pay.

☆ Offer to do the hoovering for your mum if she pays you. When she's out of the room, turn on the hoover, then settle down in a comfy chair with your favourite comic.

☆ Hide the TV remote. Suggest to your parents that they pay a pound to whoever finds it. Then – yippee! – it just happens to be you.

☆ Get your parents to pay you for eating all of your vegetables. They'll be so delighted you're going to eat healthily that they'll agree. Then, at tea time, when no one is looking, sneak the vegetables under the table, into your pockets and later into the bin.

☆ Tell your friends that you can make coins vanish. When they hand over their money, sneak it into your pockets, then shout, 'Abracadabra! It's magic – your money has vanished!' When they ask you to make it reappear, just say you haven't learned that part of the trick yet.

☆ Collect all the fruit and vegetables from your kitchen and set up a stall outside your house, with a poster reading – 'Home-Grown Organic Fruit and Veg'.

FOLLOW THE FOOTPRINTS

'Frosty Freeze are having a best snowman competition,' said Moody Margaret, glaring. 'The winner gets a year's free supply of ice cream.'

Read the full story in *Horrid Henry and the Abominable Snowman*.

Follow the footprints in the snow to find out who wins the ice cream. Is it Moody Margaret with her ballerina snowgirl, Horrid Henry with his abominable snowman or Perfect Peter with his bunny snowman?

HENRY'S FAVOURITE SNOWMEN

A Zombie
snowman

Fangmangler
snowman

Dracula
snowman

PETER'S FAVOURITES

Snail
snowman

Bunny
snowman

Worm
snowman

FESTIVE FEAST

Find the words in the wordsearch.
The first five left-over letters spell out
Henry's ideal Christmas lunch.

S	S	P	B	I	Z	Y	Z	S	A
A	U	T	R	A	E	K	T	P	P
U	X	T	U	K	C	U	L	R	O
S	H	Y	R	F	N	O	G	O	T
A	K	U	F	T	F	R	N	U	A
G	T	Z	S	A	A	I	B	T	T
E	V	E	R	V	T	Z	N	S	O
S	H	J	Y	P	P	P	G	G	E
C	S	P	I	N	S	R	A	P	S
S	T	O	R	R	A	C	B	F	D

TURKEY	CARROTS	SAUSAGES
STUFFING	PARSNIPS	CHESTNUTS
GRAVY	POTATOES	
SPROUTS	BACON	

Henry's feast is: __ __ __ __ __

171

MOODY MARGARET'S NO-CURRANTS CHRISTMAS CAKE

Horrid Henry and Moody Margaret agree on one thing – currants, raisins and sultanas are HORRIBLE! They don't like mince pies, Christmas pudding or Christmas cake. Here's Moody Margaret's Christmas cake with no currants and lots of chocolate.

You will need:
1 tbsp sugar
1 tbsp golden syrup
85g butter or margarine
2 tbsp cocoa
225g digestive biscuits
225g chocolate
20cm square baking tin
Plastic bag
Rolling pin
Saucepan
Bowl

Instructions:

1. Grease your tin with butter.

2. Put the biscuits inside a plastic bag and crush them with a rolling pin.

3. Put the sugar, golden syrup, cocoa and butter in a pan and ask an adult to help you melt them over a low heat.

4. Remove the pan from the heat and stir in the crushed biscuits.

5. Put the mixture into your baking tin and press down with a spoon.

6. Leave to cool in the fridge.

7. Ask an adult to help you melt the chocolate in a bowl over a pan of gently steaming water, then spread all over your biscuit cake.

8. When the chocolate has set, cut it into big pieces and enjoy!

NATIVITY NIGHTMARE

Fit all the parts of the School Christmas Play
into the criss-cross puzzle.

4 letters
Mary
Star

5 letters
Sheep
Jesus
Grass
Angel

6 letters
Joseph
Donkey

CLUE:
Fit the longest
words into the
puzzle first!

8 letters
Shepherd

9 letters
Innkeeper

A STAR iS BORN

Do you have star quality
or are you best in the back row?

CHRISTMAS BOXES

A game for two players – to play while you're waiting for your presents.

How to play

1. Draw a grid of dots, 6 dots by 6.

2. In between the dots, draw pictures of brilliant and terrible Christmas presents – like the Goo-Shooter and the socks shown below.

3. Take it in turns to draw a line between two of the dots, either horizontally or vertically.

4. When your line makes a box, write your initials in it and take another turn. See **1** below.

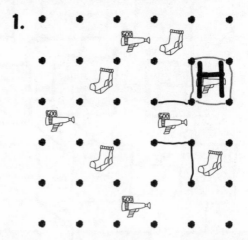

1.

Henry is using a grey pen and Peter is using a black pen. Henry has the first turn, and after four turns has already bagged himself a Goo-Shooter box. But there's still plenty of time for Peter to overtake him and win the game.

5. The game is over when all the dots are
   connected. See **2** below.

6. Count up the boxes for each player. For each
   box containing a good present, add on 5 points.
   For each box containing a bad present, take off
   5 points. The player with the highest number of
   points is the winner.

2.

The game is over! What's the score?

Peter has 13 boxes = 13
1 Goo-Shooter ADD 5 points = 18
3 Socks TAKE AWAY 15 = **3**
Better luck next time!

Henry has 12 boxes = 12
4 Goo-Shooters ADD 20 points = 34
1 Socks TAKE AWAY 5 = **29**
Well done, Henry!

CHRISTMAS CARD CONUNDRUM

Horrid Henry is the school Christmas postman. Can he deliver the right cards to the right people? Untangle the muddled-up names on each of the envelopes below.

1. GMAETARR

_ _ _ _ _ _ _ _

2. AILWMIL

_ _ _ _ _ _ _

3. PRHAL

_ _ _ _ _

4. RSM DBODOD

_ _ _ _ _ _ _ _

5. RREIUDGN

_ _ _ _ _ _ _ _

6. TBRE

_ _ _ _

EVIL ENEMIES

Henry has a lot of enemies who definitely won't be on his Christmas card list. Can you complete their names in the criss-cross below?

Across
1. SOUR _ _ _ _ _
2. PERFECT _ _ _ _ _ _
4. MOODY _ _ _ _ _ _ _ _ _
6. BOSSY _ _ _ _

Down
1. STUCK-UP _ _ _ _ _ _
3. RABID _ _ _ _ _ _ _ _
5. BOUDICCA BATTLE – _ _ _

WHAT WE LIKE BEST ABOUT CHRISTMAS

HORRID HENRY

☆ Best ☆

Getting loads of presents and eating as much chocolate as he can stuff in his mouth/ steal off the tree.

☆ Worst ☆

Having to spend his hard-earned pocket money buying OTHER people presents when they should be thrilled to receive one of Henry's drawings or poems. When will other people learn it's the thought that counts?

PERFECT PETER

☆ Best ☆

Giving loads of presents to other people and seeing their faces light up with happiness.

☆ Worst ☆

Having to watch Henry's horrible TV programmes like *Marvin the Maniac* and *Terminator Gladiator* when he just wants to enjoy *Manners with Maggie*.

MUM

☆ Best ☆

When Aunt Ruby, Stuck-Up Steve, Pimply Paul, Prissy Polly and Vomiting Vera leave.

☆ Worst ☆

Shouting at Henry all day, making sure Grandpa doesn't catch fire, cleaning up after Vomiting Vera.

DAD

☆ Best ☆

Doing lots of cooking and falling asleep in front of the telly.

☆ Worst ☆

Trying to stop Granny telling him how to peel sprouts, roast potatoes and make bread sauce.

RICH AUNT RUBY

☆ **Best** ☆
Watching Steve
spend all day
unwrapping his
presents.
☆ **Worst** ☆
Watching
Steve brag
about his
presents and trying to stop
him and Henry fighting.

STUCK-UP STEVE

☆ **Best** ☆
Getting more presents
than anyone else.
☆ **Worst** ☆
Being related to Henry.

GRANNY

☆ **Best** ☆
Telling her son that he is
doing everything wrong,
and not having to cook
Christmas dinner.
☆ **Worst** ☆
Receiving a shower cap and
a bumper pack of
dusters as a present,
when what she
really wanted was
a pair of red high
heels.

MOODY MARGARET

☆ **Best** ☆
Having her parents
do what she tells
them all day.
☆ **Worst** ☆
Going back to school
when Christmas is
over.

MISS BATTLE-AXE

☆ **Best** ☆
Watching musicals on
TV all day long.
☆ **Worst** ☆
Knowing Henry will
still be in her class when
school starts.

NAUGHTY NAMES

Henry has changed the name tags on Peter's presents to the nicknames listed below instead. Can you find them all in the wordsearch?

POOPSICLE
UGLY
BABY
SMELLY TOAD
WORM

DUKE OF POOP
NAPPY FACE
TOAD
UGG
WIBBLE PANTS

D	U	R	E	B	Q	A	N	I	E	W
A	G	G	N	A	L	N	T	L	I	I
O	I	G	L	B	C	O	C	B	S	K
T	I	P	U	Y	A	I	B	G	S	X
Y	Y	M	Q	D	S	L	R	B	U	Q
L	C	V	R	P	E	M	R	O	W	X
L	P	O	O	P	F	O	E	K	U	D
E	U	O	A	M	Z	K	I	E	C	O
M	P	N	A	P	P	Y	F	A	C	E
S	T	O	N	C	S	X	I	I	K	A
S	T	C	D	Q	P	V	K	T	X	F

HORRiD HENRY'S CHRiSTMAS RULES

☆ Getting is better than giving.

☆ Save up your pocket money – then spend it on yourself.

☆ Worms don't get presents.

☆ Beware the wrinklies – currants, raisins and grandparents.

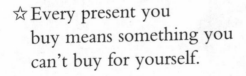

☆ Sprouts make you bald.

☆ Every present you buy means something you can't buy for yourself.

☆ I want … gets.

☆ Satsumas are NOT presents.

HORRiD HENRY'S WORST CHRISTMAS

This is the Christmas I hope I never, EVER have . . .

⭐ No presents except a pencil set, socks and bubble bath.

⭐ The only TV shows are repeats of *Daffy and her Dancing Daisies* and *Nellie's Nursery*.

⭐ Christmas lunch is just sprouts.

⭐ Stuck-up Steve is staying over.

Great Aunt Greta
sends me a pink,
sparkling handbag
and Peter £25.

Moody Margaret
comes over to
brag about all
the toys and
loot she got.

The fortune inside my
cracker says, 'You are
so lucky to have such
a wonderful brother.'

CHAMPION CHOCOLATE

Henry LOVES chocolate – and Christmas is all about eating as much of it as possible! Next time you're stealing a chocolate off the tree, distract your family with these yummy facts.

☆ In the UK, we eat £**4.3 billion** worth of chocolate a year, which is about **11 kilograms** each, the same weight as **11** bags of sugar!

☆ The word chocolate comes from the Mexican word **xocolatl**, which means 'bitter water'.

☆ In the sixteenth century, a Spanish explorer brought chocolate from **Mexico** to King Charles V of Spain in the form of **cocoa beans**. Chocolate was soon popular in Spain as a hot chocolate drink.

☆ Over **1,400** years ago, the Mayan and Aztec people in Mexico used cocoa beans as **money**. A large tomato was worth **one** cocoa bean, a rabbit **ten** beans, and a slave was worth a **hundred** beans.

☆ Chocolate cheers us up! As well as tasting yummy, it releases **endorphins** in our brains, which makes us feel happy.

☆ Eating **one small square** of dark chocolate a day is good for your heart. It contains **flavanols** that help to keep your blood pumping happily around your body.

☆ Chocolate is **poisonous** to dogs. Some of the chemicals in chocolate can make a dog's heart race so fast that it could have a seizure. The smaller the dog, the more dangerous it is to give it chocolate.

☆ Did you know you can buy **meat-flavoured** chocolate? It's made from dark chocolate and ground-up salty dried meat.

☆ Other weird and wonderful flavours of chocolate include **pepper**, **chilli**, **cauliflower**, and **basil and tomato**.

☆ The average chocolate bar contains **eight** insect legs, which have fallen in accidentally. Gross!

CHRISTMAS EVE ACTION PLAN

Henry isn't leaving anything to chance this year – here's his fool-proof list of tricks to ambush Santa and demand the loot he deserves.

Sneak up to bed early to set my traps, tee hee!	
Put a bucket of water above my bedroom door to land on Santa's head	
Stretch a skipping rope across the door entrance to trip up Santa	
Create a web of string from door to bed, and thread it with bells (to make lots of noise when Santa trips up!)	
Scatter whoopee cushions across the floor – to make even more noise!	
Leave my Super-Soaker by the bed, ready to hold Santa hostage	
Keep Mum or Dad out of my room so they don't destroy my carefully-laid Santa traps	
Double-check that Father Christmas hasn't sneaked in already and filled my stocking downstairs	

When Santa arrives, I'll hold him hostage and go through his present sack to find all the toys I want. What a brilliant plan! Now all I have to do is stay awake and wait . . .

MERRY MYSTERY

Two parcels have arrived for Henry and Peter. Can you help Henry get the present he wants? In each of the boxes, cross out the letters that appear three times. Rearrange the remaining letters to find out what's inside.

Answer: _ _ _ _

Answer: _ _ _

MISS LOVELY'S SNOWFLAKES

You will need:
A square piece of
white paper
Scissors
Sticky tape
Pencil
Ruler

MISS LOVELY'S TIP:
If you want a sparkly
snowflake, paint it
with craft glue and
sprinkle with glitter.
Even lovelier!

Instructions:

1. Fold the square piece of paper in half diagonally, so you get a triangle shape.
2. Fold this triangle in half again so you get a smaller triangle.
3. Fold this triangle into thirds. You can use a pencil and ruler to separate the triangle equally and use the lines you have drawn as a guide for folding. You should be left with a fan shape, as seen below.
4. Fold the right third over.
5. Then fold the left third over too. 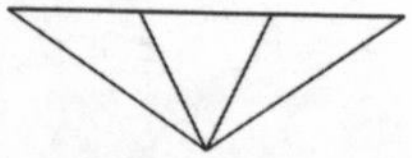
6. Cut the jagged end of your shape off, making sure to cut at an angle for the points of your snowflake.
7. Snip some fun shapes into your triangle – these will be your snowflake's pattern.
8. Now unfold your beautiful snowflake.
9. Fasten your snowflakes to the window with sticky tape. Lovely!

ULTIMATE CHRISTMAS LIST

Horrid Henry wants the best Christmas presents EVER this year. Find the items from his present list in the word search. The remaining letters spell out what his mum really buys him.

TELEVISION   **SNAKE**   **SPEEDBOAT**
CASTLE   **GUITAR**   **HELICOPTER**
MOTORBIKE   **DRUMKIT**   **COMPUTER**

S	P	E	E	D	B	O	A	T	N
C	J	R	K	I	G	S	A	O	M
A	W	A	A	P	U	Z	I	O	Z
S	L	T	N	E	V	S	T	E	S
T	T	I	S	S	I	O	A	N	D
L	H	U	A	V	R	N	D	K	E
E	R	G	E	B	C	H	I	E	F
H	E	L	I	C	O	P	T	E	R
S	E	K	T	I	K	M	U	R	D
T	E	C	O	M	P	U	T	E	R

What does Mum really buy for Henry?

_ _ _ _ _   _ _ _ _ _ _ _,   _ _ _ _ _   _ _ _

_ _ _ _ _ _ _ _ _ _ _ _ _

MAGIC MARTHA'S MERRY MAGIC

Waiting for Christmas lunch is
SO BORING! Wow your family
with magic tricks while you wait –
and make sure to charge everyone
£1 each to watch!

You will need:
Ten pieces of paper –
   all the same size
Pencil
Hat or bowl

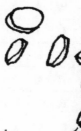

MIND READING
No one believes Magic Martha
when she says she can read minds –
until they see her do this trick!

Instructions:

1. Ask your audience to call out ten names from the Horrid Henry books.

2. Write down each name, then fold up the paper and put it in the hat. But – and this is the trick – don't really write down all the names. Only write down the first name called out – maybe it was BEEFY BERT – on all ten pieces of paper.

3. Ask a volunteer to come and pick out one of the pieces of paper from the hat. Tell them to read the name, but not to tell anyone what it is.

4. Now tell the audience that you are going to read your volunteer's mind. Ask your volunteer to concentrate very hard on the name, and look as though you're concentrating very hard too.

5. After a few seconds, announce to the audience that the name is BEEFY BERT!

JACK ATTACK

This is one of Magic Martha's
favourite card tricks.

You will need: A pack of cards.

Instructions:

1. Before you start, place one Jack at the top of the pack.

2. In front of your audience, search through the pack of cards for the other three Jacks. Leave the Jack you prepared earlier on the top and just show the other three to your audience.

3. Tell the audience that you are going to split up these three Jacks. Put one Jack on the top of the pack, another Jack on the bottom and the last Jack somewhere in the middle.

4. Place the cards on the table and invite a volunteer to come and cut the pack. Now, the bottom section of cards will be at the top of the pack.

5. Ask your volunteer to look through the pack, and tell the audience to shout 'Jack Attack!'. Your volunteer will find three Jacks together in the same place.

PRESENT PAIRS

Mum gives Dad some flowery oven gloves for Christmas. Find the three matching pairs.

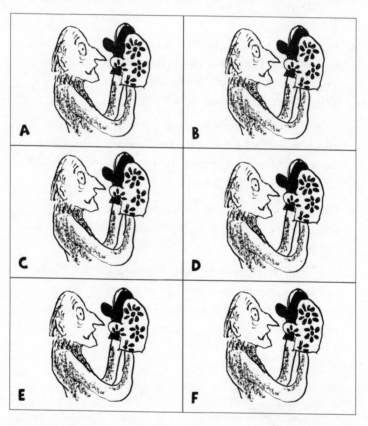

The three pairs are:

__ and __ , __ and __ , __ and __

NAUGHTY OR NICE?

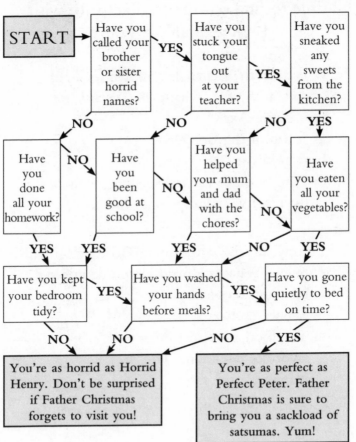

START

Have you called your brother or sister horrid names? **YES** →

Have you stuck your tongue out at your teacher? **YES** →

Have you sneaked any sweets from the kitchen?

NO ↓ **NO** ↓ **NO** ↓ **YES** ↓

Have you done all your homework?

NO → Have you been good at school?

Have you helped your mum and dad with the chores?

Have you eaten all your vegetables?

NO →

YES ↓ **YES** ↓ **NO** → **YES** ↓

Have you kept your bedroom tidy? **YES** →

Have you washed your hands before meals? **YES** →

Have you gone quietly to bed on time?

NO ↓ **NO** ↓ **NO** → **YES** ↓

You're as horrid as Horrid Henry. Don't be surprised if Father Christmas forgets to visit you!

You're as perfect as Perfect Peter. Father Christmas is sure to bring you a sackload of satsumas. Yum!

197

BRAINY BRIAN'S BIG END OF THE YEAR QUIZ

So you think you know everything there is to know about Horrid Henry? Now it's time to find out the terrible truth with Brainy Brian's big quiz!

1. When Horrid Henry gets all five spellings correct in the test, what is his reward from Miss Battle-Axe?
   (a) A bag of Big Boppers
   (b) A gold star
   (c) Promotion to the top spelling group and twenty-five extra spellings to learn

2. 'Lumpy surprise with lumps. Gristly glop with globules.' What is Horrid Henry describing?
   (a) His mum's cooking
   (b) School dinners
   (c) The food at Perfect Peter's favourite restaurant, The Happy Carrot

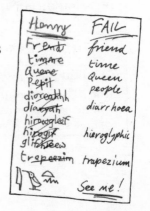

3. Where does Horrid Henry save his pocket money?
   (a) In a skeleton bank
   (b) In a piggy bank
   (c) Under his pillow

4. Horrid Henry is banned from trick or treating
   on Halloween because . . .
   (a) His mum and dad don't want him to eat too
       many sweets
   (b) He cut off lots of Perfect Peter's hair
   (c) He's eaten all the satsumas his mum and dad
       bought for treats

5. Where does Perfect Peter hide his diary?
   (a) On his bookshelf, between The Happy Nappy
       and The Hoppy Hippo
   (b) In a pirate chest, buried in the garden
   (c) In his pants drawer

6. When Dad asks Horrid Henry to name a vegetable he likes, what does Henry say?
(a) Cauliflower
(b) Sprouts
(c) Crisps

7. When they go shopping, why doesn't Henry want his mum to buy him a pair of pink and green trousers?
(a) They're girls' trousers
(b) They're too tight
(c) They're too expensive

8. When his mum gives him a large cardboard box, what does Henry make out of it?
(a) A sweet little house
(b) A time machine
(c) A den for the Purple Hand Club

9. There's only one vegetable that Perfect Peter
   doesn't like.

   Do you know what it is?

   (a) Beetroot

   (b) Sprouts

   (c) Cabbage

10. What is Horrid Henry's favourite board game
    called?

    (a) Winna

    (b) Gotcha

    (c) Betcha

How did you do? Turn to the answer section at the back to
find out.

7 — 10

You deserve to hold your head high. All that hard work
reading lots of Horrid Henry books has definitely paid off. A
year well spent!

4 — 6

Nothing to cheer about, but there's still hope. Pull up your
socks, put in a few more reading hours, and you're sure to get
a better score next year.

1 — 3

What have you been doing all year?

TOP TEN TRIUMPHS OF THE YEAR

Henry has had a brilliant year –
check out his best moments below.

1. Sneaked 865 sweets.

2. Did NOT do 15 pieces of homework.

3. Pinched Peter 250 times without Mum noticing.

4. Tricked Moody Margaret 100 times.

5. Tricked 3 Gold Gizmos off Peter.

6. Defeated the Demon Dinner Lady.

7. Was the best Innkeeper ever in the school Xmas play.

8. Persuaded Mum to buy me Root-A-Toot trainers.

9. Gave away all my nits.

10. Dropped ten million billion zillion peas on the floor.

Can you write down your own top ten triumphs?

1. _____

2. _____

3. _____

4. _____

5. _____

6. _____

7. _____

8. _____

9. _____

10. _____

Merry Christmas
and a
Happy New Year
from
Horrid Henry!

Stumped?

For answers to all the puzzles in this book, turn the page!

ANSWERS

p153 Seasonal Splits

This tastes yummy with gravy and stuffing	TUR	KEY
People come to your door and sing these	CAR	OLS
There are usually lots of these in the school nativity	ANG	ELS
Father Christmas travels on one of these	SLE	IGH
This can be used to decorate your tree	TIN	SEL
This forms when it's very cold	ICI	CLE
You'll need to wear these when you go outside	GLO	VES
Henry thinks this is one of the worst gifts EVER!	JUM	PER

p162-163 Christmas Concert Criss-Cross

p166

Perfect Peter and his bunny

p169 Festive Feast

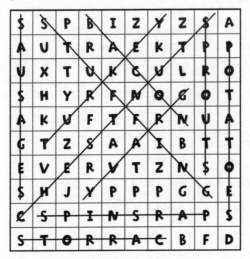

Henry's feast is: PIZZA

p170 Nativity Nightmare

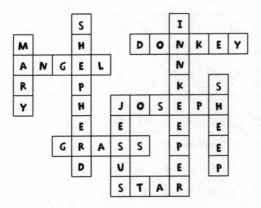

p174 Christmas Card Conundrum

1. Margaret   2. William   3. Ralph
4. Mrs Oddbod   5. Gurinder   6. Bert

209

p175 Evil Enemies

Across
1. SOUR SUSAN
2. PERFECT PETER
4. MOODY MARGARET
6. BOSSY BILL

Down
1. STUCK-UP STEVE
3. RABID REBECCA
5. BOUDICCA BATTLE – AXE

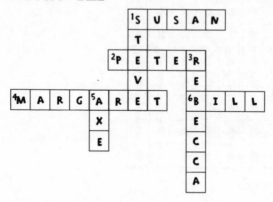

p178 Naughty Names

D	U	R	E	B	Q	A	N	I	E	W
A	G	G	N	A	L	N	T	L	I	I
O	I	G	L	B	C	O	C	B	S	K
T	I	P	U	X	A	I	B	G	S	X
Y	Y	M	Q	D	S	L	R	B	U	Q
L	C	V	R	P	E	M	R	O	W	X
L	P	O	O	F	F	O	E	K	U	D
E	U	O	A	M	Z	K	I	E	C	O
M	P	N	A	P	P	Y	F	A	C	E
S	T	O	N	C	S	X	I	I	K	A
S	T	C	D	Q	P	V	K	T	X	F

210

p185 Merry Mystery

1. DOLL   2. GOO

p187 Ultimate Christmas List

```
S P E E D B O A T N
C J R K I G S A O M
A W A A P U Z I O Z
S L T N E V S T E S
T T I S S I O A N D
L H U A V R N D K E
E R C E B C H I E F
H E L I C O P T E R
S E K T I K M U R D
A E C O M P U T E R
```

Henry's mum buys him
JIGSAW PUZZLE, VESTS AND HANDKERCHIEFS

p190 Present Pairs

The three pairs are:
A and E
B and C (one less petal on the middle flower)
D and F (one petal more on top flower)

p192-193 Brainy Brian's Big End of year Quiz

1. (c)   2. (b)   3. (a)   4. (b)   5. (a)
6. (c)   7. (a)   8. (b)   9. (a)   10. (b)

211

Storybooks

Horrid Henry
Horrid Henry and the Secret Club
Horrid Henry Tricks the Tooth Fairy
Horrid Henry's Nits
Horrid Henry Gets Rich Quick
Horrid Henry's Haunted House
Horrid Henry and the Mummy's Curse
Horrid Henry's Revenge
Horrid Henry and the Bogey Babysitter
Horrid Henry's Stinkbomb
Horrid Henry's Underpants
Horrid Henry Meets the Queen
Horrid Henry and the Mega-Mean Time Machine
Horrid Henry and the Football Fiend
Horrid Henry's Christmas Cracker
Horrid Henry and the Abominable Snowman
Horrid Henry Robs the Bank
Horrid Henry Wakes the Dead
Horrid Henry Rocks
Horrid Henry and the Zombie Vampire
Horrid Henry's Monster Movie
Horrid Henry's Nightmare
Horrid Henry's Guide to Perfect Parents
Horrid Henry's Krazy Ketchup
Horrid Henry's Cannibal Curse

Early Readers

Colour books

Horrid Henry's Big Bad Book
Horrid Henry's Wicked Ways
Horrid Henry's Evil Enemies
Horrid Henry Rules the World
Horrid Henry's House of Horrors
Horrid Henry's Dreadful Deeds
Horrid Henry Shows Who's Boss
Horrid Henry's A-Z of Everything Horrid
Horrid Henry Fearsome Four
Horrid Henry's Royal Riot
Horrid Henry's Tricky Tricks
Horrid Henry's Lucky Dip

Joke Books

Horrid Henry's Joke Book
Horrid Henry's Jolly Joke Book
Horrid Henry's Mighty Joke Book
Horrid Henry versus Moody Margaret
Horrid Henry's Hilariously Horrid Joke Book
Horrid Henry's Purple Hand Gang Joke Book
Horrid Henry's All Time Favourite Joke Book
Horrid Henry's Jumbo Joke Book

Activity books

Horrid Henry's Brainbusters
Horrid Henry's Headscratchers
Horrid Henry's Mindbenders
Horrid Henry's Colouring Book
Horrid Henry's Puzzle Book
Horrid Henry's Sticker Book
Horrid Henry Runs Riot
Horrid Henry's Classroom Chaos
Horrid Henry's Holiday Havoc
Horrid Henry's Wicked Wordsearches
Horrid Henry's Mad Mazes
Horrid Henry's Crazy Crosswords
Horrid Henry's Big Bad Puzzle Book
Horrid Henry's Gold Medal Games
Where's Horrid Henry?
Horrid Henry's Crafty Christmas
Where's Horrid Henry Colouring Book

Fact Books

Horrid Henry's Ghosts
Horrid Henry's Dinosaurs
Horrid Henry's Sports
Horrid Henry's Food
Horrid Henry's King and Queens
Horrid Henry's Bugs
Horrid Henry's Bodies
Horrid Henry's Animals
Horrid Henry's Space
Horrid Henry's Crazy Creatures

Visit Horrid Henry's website at
www.horridhenry.co.uk for competitions,
games, downloads and a monthly newsletter